CASTLE BUTTE

CASTLE BUTTE

JOHN D. NESBITT

FIVE STAR
A part of Gale, a Cengage Company

Farmington Hills, Mich • San Francisco • New York • Waterville, Maine
Meriden, Conn • Mason, Ohio • Chicago

LIBRARY OF CONGRESS CATALOGING-IN-PUBLICATION DATA

Names: Nesbitt, John D., author.
Title: Castle Butte / John D. Nesbitt.
Description: First edition. | Farmington Hills, Mich. : Five Star, a part of Gale Cengage Learning, [2018]
Identifiers: LCCN 2017053604 (print) | LCCN 2018000887 (ebook) | ISBN 9781432842826 (ebook) | ISBN 9781432842819 (ebook) | ISBN 9781432842802 (hardcover)
Subjects: | CYAC: Frontier and pioneer life—Wyoming—Fiction. | Wyoming—History—19th century—Fiction. | BISAC: FICTION / Historical. | FICTION / Westerns.
Classification: LCC PZ7.1.N465 (ebook) | LCC PZ7.1.N465 Cas 2018 (print) | DDC [Fic]—dc23
LC record available at https://lccn.loc.gov/2017053604

First Edition. First Printing: May 2018
Find us on Facebook–https://www.facebook.com/FiveStarCengage
Visit our website–http://www.gale.cengage.com/fivestar/
Contact Five Star™ Publishing at FiveStar@cengage.com

For Kathy Skala,
our beloved classmate.

CHAPTER ONE

Castle Butte stood out clear against a midsummer sky, dark and steadfast with a bright blue background. As Alden rode up the slope toward its base, the solid formation loomed above and showed itself to be much larger than it seemed from a distance. Dark trees, pine and cedar, grew out of the rock and earth of the sides. A ridge of stone turrets and ramparts lined the crown, and more trees rose from the level area on top. Some of the trees grew in masses, while others stood by themselves and gave the illusion of people looking out and waving at the plains below. To the left of the butte, a narrow ridge led up in long, wavy steps, and along the spine of the grassy ridge, other individual trees stood in profile. They, too, resembled humans, walking up to join their friends.

Alden's horse, Badger, stopped and turned on a level spot, blew out a breath, and shook his head. Alden patted the horse on the neck and gazed downslope to the left, where the small herd of stock was grazing. Badger knew the routine. At this time of day, Alden rode around to the far edge of the herd and began to haze the animals toward town.

Alden glanced again at the butte. The illusion of people dancing and waving was gone. But the butte itself, with its perfect arrangement of earth and rocks and trees, perfect because it emerged from the forces of nature itself, was durable and reassuring.

"Yep, yep," said Alden. "Time to go back." He leaned in the

saddle as Badger began to pick his way down the slope toward the scattering of animals.

The town herd, as it was called, consisted of nine milk cows, five calves, four yearling heifers, and a small, cream-colored mule. Nineteen in all, shifting and wandering this way and that. Alden counted them for the hundredth time that day as he began to push them into a group. One of the cows, a large Jersey, had a bell. She took the lead as the others formed a loose group and began plodding.

Alden imagined the minds of the dull animals, each thinking about its pen or shed. Some of the cows were ready to be milked. Most if not all of the animals would be thinking about hay or grain. Even the mule, which went by the name of Princess and was said to be smart, would not have a sense of days ahead or days behind. Alden had read that several features put men above other animals: the human ability to make fire, to cook, to make tools, to measure time, to buy and sell, to think and reason, and to record thoughts. A person might have one cow, two cows, a thousand, or none. And unlike any cow or mule, which did not have possessions, some men coveted what others had.

Alden touched his heels to Badger, and the horse took off to bring a straying heifer back into the group. So much for daydreaming, Alden thought. Work was work, and he needed to make sure these animals returned to their owners.

He counted the herd again and looked it over without much thought. From the hooves of the nearest cow, small bits of dry grass rose and then fell. The grass was beginning to dry.

Alden took a broad look at the surrounding country. He saw what he had registered before but had not announced to himself. The green grass of early summer was giving way to lighter tones. Time marched on. Now that he thought of it, he had seen two or three full-grown grasshoppers showing their wings, some yellow and some orange, as they whirred away. The grasshoppers were the size of a slender rifle cartridge. Earlier in the season, they had been no longer than a fingernail.

Alden had trailed the animals for less than a mile when Badger's ears went up and his head turned. Off to Alden's right, a man was riding from the southwest. Alden slacked his reins and let the herd animals slow down and graze. He thought the rider might cross ahead of them, but the man changed his course and rode toward Alden.

As the horse and rider drew closer, Alden looked for familiar features and saw none. The man had pale-colored hair topped by a black hat. He wore a greyish-tan linen duster, unbuttoned, and he had a duffel bag tied to the back of his saddle. The horse was a plain-looking, dark animal with no markings.

The man slowed the horse and came to a stop about fifteen feet away. He took off his lightweight leather riding gloves and set them on the saddle in front of him. Flexing his fingers, he said, "Warm day."

"Yes, it is."

The man drew out a folded white handkerchief and wiped his face. When he was done, Alden noticed that he had a bird-like nose, flattened downward, and a spare, pale mustache. The man put away the handkerchief and pulled on his gloves.

"Who do you work for?" he asked.

"People in town. I take this herd out every day."

"Town's over there, I'd guess."

"That's right."

"How far is it to Silver Springs?"

"At least fifteen miles, I think." Alden pointed toward the east. "It's on the other side of that line of hills. There's a couple of different trails that go through."

"I know."

Alden wondered why the traveler had to ask about the distance if he knew about the trails.

The man turned his head in a slow, downward direction as he regarded the herd animals. "Milk cows," he said.

"Some of them."

"Well, it keeps you out of trouble, kid."

Just as Alden knew better than to ask questions of a stranger, he knew better than to talk back. He took refuge in a saying he had heard a hundred times. "All work is good work."

"Isn't that the honest truth?" The man stretched his upper lip and rubbed his mustache with his gloved hand. "Well, I've got to be movin'. Take good care of these cows." He set off on a course that would take him north of town about a mile.

Alden watched the man ride away. He was a self-assured, confident fellow, old enough to talk down to Alden. Maybe thirty. He seemed like someone on the lookout for opportunity. Most of the homesteading tracts had been taken up, but some of those had changed hands already or were available to be bought, and Alden had heard that other areas might open up in the near future. Free land brought people of different kinds, from dirt-grubbing farmers who worked like insects to adventurers who liked to build, buy, sell, and live off their wits. Alden's sense of the pale-haired stranger was that he would be the type who thought he was a little smarter than the next fellow. On the other hand, he might not be looking for land or opportunity. Maybe he was just riding through.

At the edge of town, some of the animals dispersed in the directions of their homes. Princess, the cream-colored mule, picked up her feet and trotted ahead, turning into an alley. Alden followed, swishing his rope and clucking, as he pushed Julia Redwine's Jersey cow to its corral. Princess stood in her pen with the gate open and watched as the cow lumbered on with Badger and Alden at its heels.

Julia appeared in the alleyway, pulling the gate outward and standing to block the way. Her brown hair, pinned up neat, shone in the sun, and she was wearing her white store apron.

"Hee-ya!" Alden called, and the cow turned into its pen.

Julia closed the gate and stood by, shading her eyes with her hand. "Thank you," she said.

"You're welcome." Not knowing what else to say, he added, "Another day."

"She didn't give you any trouble?"

"Not today. She stayed with the herd."

"That's good." Julia smiled as she lowered her hand. Her blue eyes sparkled. "A boy and his horse. You do your work well."

Alden touched his hat brim. "Thank you." He nudged his heel against Badger and moved on, glad as always to have the cow back in its pen with no extra worry for the owner. Julia had more than enough to do. She was a worker. Not everyone was. With her husband dead and gone at a young age, she ran the store and took care of her two children. The cow was enough of a nuisance that Julia had to look after it herself, penning it up and milking it, in addition to everything else. Still, she had time for a good word.

Alden rode down the alley, turned right, and arrived at the main street. There he paused, looking up and down the thoroughfare. None of the animals were wandering around, so he considered his day's work done. A boy's work, tending the town herd. It paid wages, though not much, and he had his own obligations. An image of his father rose in his mind, and he brushed it away.

Alden was about to ride onto the main street when he saw a ranch wagon coming his way and beginning to turn left in front of him. He drew rein and waited.

The wagon was drawn by two dark horses that huffed and snorted as they pulled into the turn. Alden observed the driver, a hard-looking man with a black hat, dark hair and brows, dark eyes, and a black neckerchief. His face showed creases as he handled the reins and leaned in the seat.

Next to the man on the bench, as the wagon swung around, a second person came into view, also dressed in work clothes. Alden was not sure of the person at first, because of the hat and denim trousers, but as the wagon turned, he saw a girl's long, dark-brown hair tied back and spreading out below her shoulders. She was about Alden's age, with dark eyes and a clear, open expression. She met his gaze and held it, turning her head and then her upper body.

The man spoke, the wagon jolted, the girl shifted, and the rear wheel came into view. The outfit rolled away, raising dust, and Alden could see nothing more detailed than the backs of two people on a wagon seat.

Alden waited a minute to let the dust settle before he nudged his horse out onto the main street. Badger took it slow, ambling west. Out of habit, Alden looked down to watch his horse's feet and to see that no straps or saddle gear hung loose. When he raised his eyes, the ranch wagon was gone from view. He rolled a glance to his left to see if he could catch a glimpse of someone he knew through the windows of the dining room of the Landmark Hotel. No blond hair showed. He turned left at the next corner, turned again into the alley, and rode past the back door of the hotel. It was closed. For all he knew, Claudette was right inside, hashing in the kitchen, but he would have to wait until another day.

At the end of the alley he took a deep breath, turned right, and headed toward home. Half a block later, he remembered to water his horse, so he reined Badger around and rode back to the main street. Turning right where the bank sat cater-cornered from the hotel, he rode east two blocks to the edge of town. The way station was closed up, but the wooden trough in front had a still surface of dark water a few inches from the top.

Alden swung down, loosened the cinch, and let his horse drink. Late afternoon lingered, and the cool air of evening had not yet begun to move. With one hand holding the reins and the other resting on the saddle, Alden looked over his shoulder. Down the main street, a ranch wagon raised dust as it moved toward the slipping sun. A dog ran out to chase it and turned back. Alden wondered if it was the same wagon he had seen earlier. He thought it might be, as no other wagons were in sight. Then it, too, turned left and disappeared.

Alden gazed at the empty main street. Not a tree rose to the height of a building, so the small town of Morse lay in a sunny haze. A dog barked. A woman's voice sounded in the tone of a mother calling her children. The crowing of a rooster stopped short, and the town went quiet again.

Alden moved the horse away from the trough, tightened the cinch, and mounted up. Everything seemed right for the time being. He had done his work, he had remembered to water his horse, and he hadn't lollygagged in town. That didn't mean his father would be happy, but Alden was used to his father's moods.

Dusk lay heavy in the front room of the house as Alden opened the door and walked in. The smell of tobacco smoke hung in the air. As faint light spilled inward through the open doorway, Alden made out the shadowy form of his father sitting in the old stuffed chair.

"It's about time you got home. It's almost dark."

"I didn't waste any time. I had to do the chores outside." Alden hung his hat on a peg. "Where's Grant?"

"He hasn't come in yet."

"Isn't it time to light a lamp?" Alden imagined his father sitting in the chair, silent and sulking, as the daylight had faded little by little.

"Go ahead. I try to save money on kerosene, that's all."

Alden found the matches on the sideboard and lit the lamp. As the light spread, he noticed the whiskey glass on the upturned crate next to his father's chair. He was not surprised to see it, but his stomach tightened.

"A penny at a time," said the father. "Pennies make dollars." He heaved out a breath with his mouth open. "That's what it is to be poor. If you're born poor, you live that way and you die that way." He breathed again. "No one'll give a poor man a chance in life."

Alden spoke before thinking. "Some people get a chance with free land."

"Bah. Whoever said you could make a living on a hundred-and-sixty acres is either a fool or a liar. It's damn few cows you can raise on that much land. Even if you wanted to plant a crop, you can't grow spuds or wheat one year out of three. Not here, at least. You don't run the land. It runs you. As for home-steadin', someone makes money off of it, but it ain't the little man. It's the developers and the land locators. Government gets people to come out here, take up land, and try to pinch out a livin', but it's all up to them once they get here. Man tries to do better for himself, and it makes no difference. The poor man just stays poor. No one wants to help. No one."

Alden felt his blood rising. "I work."

"Sure you do. Lookin' after milk cows and readin' a book all day."

"I didn't read a book today."

"But you do. For all the good it does you."

"I still work."

"I know you do, and that's not what I was talkin' about. Of course everyone in the family works. But I meant the others.

The big outfits, they help each other, but they want the little ones to fail. Then they can grab up the land. And the government stands by and watches." The old man drew out his tobacco and papers. "You might as well get started on supper. Your brother should be here in a little while."

Alden went to work scrubbing potatoes—spuds he had bought in town with his wages. He made himself calm down. He knew it did no good to argue with his father. The old man had his opinions well-rehearsed, and he didn't want to hear anyone else's. For Alden's part, he had his ideas, but many of them had not taken clear shape. They drifted through his mind during the day, and he had not had practice expressing them. Left to himself now, he sorted through them.

At the bottom if it all, he thought there was something good, something worth working for, in having land of one's own. For someone like himself who had never had anything, land was something. Alden saw it as opportunity, while others, like his father and his brother, saw it as a burden. Alden knew of other families in which some members worked the land while others "worked out"—for other farmers or ranchers or for businesses in town.

Alden rubbed his thumb at a dark spot on the potato. He didn't think reading made the difference between valuing the land and resenting it, but he had acquired in his reading the idea that ownership of land was possible in the New World. It was democratic; it was American. More important than the level of idea, however, was the level of feeling. Alden knew he had a feeling for the land, and not everyone had it.

The father lit his cigarette and shifted in his seat. "It's not like it used to be," he said. When Alden didn't respond, his father said, "Work day and night for years, raisin' you kids, and now my energy's all gone. Worn out. I go out back and come in, and I'm winded. Have to sit down. Can't do a thing." He rubbed his thumb against his first two fingers, yellowish brown with tobacco stain. "It's hell to get old."

Alden raised his eyebrows as he took a more deliberate look at his father, sitting in the lamplight beneath a haze of smoke. With yellowed eyes and a splotchy face, the man looked old. Although Alden and his brother referred to him as the old man, just as he referred to his own father, Hiram Clare was only fifty-six years old. But his working days were over. He left all work to his boys.

"I wonder what's taking Grant so long," Alden said.

"You never know. You can't just quit at six like someone sittin' at a desk. Many's the time I came in after dark. And still had chores to do. Years and years." The old man lifted his cigarette. "Long before you kids were big enough to help. Never a hand from anyone."

"I know."

"You don't know. Your mother up and died and left me to do everything. I didn't have any help. No woman in her right mind would come out here, grub for a livin', and take care of someone else's kids. Not without gettin' paid, and I don't know anyone that ever had a homestead and could pay a housekeeper. Maybe someone in town, yeah, like the banker. I suppose you see him every day and smile."

"No, I don't."

"He's a good one. Shake your hand and squeeze your last penny out of you."

Alden said nothing.

"I could have gotten somewhere, but he wouldn't let me. Cuttin' other people's hay. But soon as I got behind on my payment, he took my sickle cutter away."

Alden nodded, having heard the story more than once before.

The old man's voice rose. "What does he know about hay?"

"I don't know."

"Or cattle? Or wheat?" The old man's voice continued to cut the air.

"I don't know that, either."

"Of course you don't. But there's no need to talk back to me."

"I was just agreeing."

"It was your tone."

Alden took a deep breath. The old man was getting worse, it seemed. He had always criticized and complained, but now he chewed things over and over. The smallest things set him off, and once he started, he wouldn't let anything go. Also of late, his voice had taken on a whine.

Alden continued with the potatoes, slicing them and cutting out bad spots. He could feel his father calming down. He stole a glance at the old man and saw his lips moving, as if he was mumbling to himself.

The old man spoke in a conversational tone. "That's the way to do it. You can't make a livin' off a section of land. But you can work from there. Cuttin' hay is one way, and buyin' and sellin' cattle is another."

"All we've done is sell."

"Of course. I know that. But we haven't grazed this place this year, and it's got some value as winter range. If we can lease it, we can use the money as a stake, build back up."

Alden could not see how the money was going to go around enough to pay the mortgage and the living expenses, much less give them a stake for another enterprise. But he saw no point in contradicting.

"That's the thing," the old man continued. "The more I think of it, the more it seems to be the way. Business. It's just that you can't get anyone to back you. So we need to do it ourselves. The lease money won't do it all. Maybe you and Grant both'll have to work out for a while."

Alden was familiar with this version of his father's thinking, also. They would all work together, save up, make a recovery, and become prosperous. When the old man spoke in this way, he seemed as if he saw a road stretching well into the future. This outlook was the other side of the coin from the pessimism he most often expressed and always returned to. So Alden sliced potatoes and said nothing.

The door opened, and Grant walked in. He was wearing a short-billed cap and his drab work clothes.

The old man's eyes opened wide. "I didn't hear you come into the yard."

"I heard you all the way from the barn." Grant hung his cap on a peg and squared his shoulders. His full head of brown hair caught the lamplight.

Alden assumed his brother was referring to the old man's ranting about the banker.

Grant continued. "Work all day, and come home to hear you from a mile away."

The father resumed his quarrelsome tone from before. "What took you so long?"

Grant turned, gave a stare with his light brown eyes, and made an expression of disgust. "What do you think? I was fixing a lousy fence."

"Nothin's that far away on this place."

"What does that matter? I have to do everything by myself—dig the postholes, tamp in posts, splice the wire, reuse old nails and steeples—all for the purpose of keeping out the neighbor's slobbering cattle."

"I've done all that myself. You're not tellin' me anything new."

"Well, I'm doin' it all now, and I get tired of it. Work all day every day on a cheap, run-down place, and I never have a dime to show for it."

"I never did, either. And here's Alden, he works out, and he doesn't get anything for himself. It all goes for the common good."

Grant raised his chin. "The common good. I've heard that forever. And I haven't gotten any good out of it."

"Not that you remember. All the time you kids were little, I worked day and night—"

"That was then. I'm not gonna work my whole life and never have a nickel. Be some dirt-grubbin' honyocker."

The old man's eyes narrowed. "Call it what you want. We stick together. I worked for you kids, and I taught you that we all work together." His lower lip trembled. "And now you throw it in my face."

"I'm not throwing anything. I'm just tired of never having a red cent, and I don't see where things'll ever be any better. Worse, if anything."

The old man pinched out the stub of his cigarette and dropped it in a sardine can. His voice rose in its whiny tone as he said, "So you don't like it, huh?"

"No, I don't."

"So that's all the thanks I get."

"Thanks? I think I've done enough. I've worked for free for as long as I can remember."

The old man's voice whined again. "And you don't like it?"

"No, I don't."

"Well, if you don't like it, you can go somewhere else and see how much better it is."

"I just might do that. I'm sick of all of this."

"Wait till you get really sick, and they treat you like an old dog."

"Oh, my God." Grant turned. "How long until supper, Alden?"

"Half an hour, maybe. I've got to slice the bacon, fry it, and fry these potatoes."

Grant nodded. "I'll be back."

"Where are you going?"

"To the room. To pack my bag."

Alden paused with the knife in his hand as Grant walked in front of their father and headed for the room the boys shared. The father had a blank expression as he turned his head and watched his son walk away.

Alden stood by as Grant saddled his horse by lantern light in the barn. "You don't have to go," Alden said.

"I'm fed up with all of this. Work forever and never have a damn thing."

"I work, too, and I don't get anything."

"That's up to you. But I'm not going to spend my whole life diggin' in the dirt. There's a world out there."

"What do you know about it?"

"So far, just what I've heard, from fellas like Penner and Sample."

"They came back, too."

"They can leave again if they want to. Same as I can now."

"See the lights of a big town."

"You'll want to do the same thing someday."

Alden shook his head. "I couldn't just walk away. I feel—"

"Stuck."

"You could call it that. But I guess I feel . . . responsible."

Grant shrugged. "Like I say, that's up to you. You can stay as long as you want, livin' on a dirt patch and workin' in a one-horse cowtown. But I'm going to see more of life."

"You'll come back, won't you?"

"To visit."

Grant tied his duffel bag onto the back of the saddle, put on the bridle, and turned the horse around.

Alden held the lantern as his older brother led the horse out of the barn. Alden had a lump in his throat as they shook hands.

"So long, kid."

"Goodbye, Grant. Come back and see us."

"You never know. I might come back with enough money to pay off the whole works."

"Do you think you would?"

"Hard to say. But I'll tell you one thing. I'm through with bein' broke all the time."

Grant mounted up and rode away in the night.

Alden carried the lantern into the barn and felt the emptiness of one horse and one person being gone. He fought the lump in his throat and held back the tears, but he had to sniff. As he took in a deep breath and blew out the light, he realized he now had the whole burden of taking care of his father and trying to save the bit of land they had.

Alden cut slices from the same slab of bacon the next evening. As he did, he listened to his father's harangue.

"Well, your brother didn't like it. Shows you how much he appreciates what anyone did for him. I tried to raise you kids with the idea that you work together and help each other out. Now he turns his back on you and me both, makes it harder on the two of us. Wants money. He's got the rest of his life to go out and chase a fortune. Fat chance he'll make anything anyway. Most kids come home broke."

"The ones that come home."

"Oh, yeah. And God help him if he gets in trouble. There's plenty of 'em does that. I hope he's got enough brains to stay away from that sort of thing, but you never know." The old man took a sip of whiskey. "Makes it rough on us, that's all I can say. I don't know what we're goin' to do without him." The father's lip trembled. "I counted on him. I had hopes for him. And then he walks out on us."

Alden did not say anything. In all their years of growing up, Grant had been number one, and Alden had been number two. The old man always swore he did not have a favorite, but anyone could see it. The old man's sister, Aunt Em, who had come to stay for a while, had remarked on it, and the old man had gone into a fury. Now his elder son had left him, and the wound ran deep.

The old man took refuge in complaining. "He'll see how easy it is to make it on his own. Nothin's free. Say what he will, he never went hungry at home, and he always had a roof over his head. Maybe he'll appreciate it when he doesn't have it anymore. Maybe he'll see that he's not any better than the rest of us. It might do him some good." The old man heaved a breath. "But to walk out on us the way he did, I just can't take it."

Alden could imagine a word or two in favor of the son who did not walk out, but he did not expect to hear them.

CHAPTER TWO

Alden sat in the shade of his horse as the town herd grazed downslope to the north. At this angle, he could count the animals without difficulty. He also had a good view of the surrounding country, a vast grassland that stretched away in all directions. To the west, the Laramie Mountains rose in a purplish-blue haze, more than a day's ride away. To the north, closer but still a half-day's ride, a line of high, treeless, rolling hills ran from west to east and faded into the plains. A mile or so farther to the east, less than ten miles from where he sat, a row of dry hills, with thinner grass and a sparse scattering of trees, ran from north to south. In back of him, to the south, lay a stretch of land he could not see because of the hill he sat on. It was a district he could envision well, south and west of his family's place. Poorer range, it consisted of breaks and hardscrabble homesteads up against a line of barren hills that reached halfway to the Laramie Mountains.

For a boy sitting next to his horse, this was a vast country, somewhere between five hundred and a thousand square miles. From maps he had seen and books he had read, he knew the American West ran for a thousand miles in all directions. He was in big country in an enormous region, where ranches had tens of thousands of acres, and he had heard how a person could ride for days and never come to a fence.

From where he sat, he could picture his family's homestead, over the hill and a little more than five miles away. For as much as he tired of his father's carping, the old man was right. This country did not favor the little man, and a hundred-and-sixty acres of dry land was next to impossible to make a living on. Even a section, a square mile with six-hundred-and-forty acres, was a mere dab in a range of sagebrush and grassland. His father had worked hard, starting with a quarter-section and acquiring others as his neighbors gave up. Now he had a full section, but all of it was mortgaged.

One time, when Alden was ten years old, he was sitting in the general store waiting for his father, when he overhead a man talking to the storekeeper.

The man said, "I'm land poor, that's what I am. I've got more than three thousand acres, and I can't afford to make a livin' off of it."

Alden had pondered the saying for several years until it began to make sense. Now that he worked on his own and saw what he was faced with at home, he could understand "land poor" in his own terms. Still, he went back to the idea that having land of one's own was worth working for.

The herd of town animals moved west as it grazed over a low hill and moved down the other side. Alden checked his cinch and mounted up. Cresting the hill, he saw Castle Butte less than a mile away. He kept his eye on the herd as Badger picked his way along. The sun hung bright in the sky above the butte. In another hour it would begin to slip, and Alden could turn the herd around.

Badger stopped and raised his head to the left. Alden followed the line of sight up the grassy hillside and stopped at a buck antelope in profile.

The animal had appeared out of nowhere, as antelope seemed to do. Its hide was pale tan and white in the afternoon sunlight, and its horns had the dull color of charcoal. The animal was husky and handsome, his horns rising as far above his forehead as his nose reached down below. He stood motionless, gazing in the curious way antelope had. Then he turned and walked along the hillside toward the butte, in no hurry.

On this peaceful, sunny afternoon, Alden wished him well. Out on the public domain, there was room for everyone—the town animals that would go back to their pens, the wild animal that knew no property lines and avoided fences, and the human who could imagine meeting such an antelope in the cooler part of the year.

Princess, the cream-colored mule, trotted to her pen as usual, and Julia Redwine's cow went into her corral without any trouble. With his day's work done, Alden watered his horse and rinsed his face. In the saddle again, he rode to the center of town and turned left where the Landmark Hotel sat on the corner. Down the side street and into the alley, he dismounted.

The back door of the hotel was open. Sounds from the kitchen reached him—voices, the banging of a pot. The odor of fried meat floated on the air. Alden loitered, walking a few yards one way and then the other, reins in hand.

A flash of white caught his eye. A couple of minutes later, a human form appeared in the doorway. The white apron and blond hair proved to be Claudette as she stepped outside. His pulse jumped. The apron was tied snug, and it did not conceal her figure.

She moved toward him in quick steps, brushing back her hair with one hand. In a low voice she said, "Why do you always come by when I'm busy?"

"It's the only time I can. I bring in the herd, and I've got but a few minutes before I have to go home. At least I was able to see you today."

Her brown eyes roved over him. "It's been a while."

"I've come by, but the door is always closed."

"This is the busiest time of day. You know that."

"It's the only time I've got right now." He realized they were both repeating themselves, and he hesitated before the next thing he had to say. "Grant left home. I don't know if you heard that."

She held her eyes on him. "No, I didn't. What does that mean for you?"

"For right now, it means that I've got less free time than ever." He put his hand on her hip, touching the fabric of her apron. "I've been dying to see you."

She took his hand away, then drew in a breath that made her bosom rise. "I've been hoping to see you, too. Working here is just as bad as being on the farm. I work breakfast, dinner, and supper."

"Even if I could come by at a different time, when would that be?"

Her brown eyes held steady. "It would have to be later, after ten."

"I would have to ride back into town. I don't know if I could do that. Especially now, with Grant gone, and the old man—"

"That's why people leave home. It's just that in my case, I went from one kind of a jail to another, and all my wages go home."

"Every cent?"

"Just about. I tell you, it's almost as bad as the farm. I don't blame your brother. I'm ready to do something myself."

Alden drew his brows together. "I couldn't see leaving home, running away."

"Depends on whether you want to be treated like a kid forever, and besides, you don't have to run away."

"What do you do?"

She held her eyes on him again, as if she had to tell him

everything but was willing to do so. "You set up your own house."

He had to swallow. "I don't think I'm ready for that yet."

She shifted her body and held up her chin. "Well, no one's forcing you."

He moved toward her and met her in a kiss. A tingling wave went through him, and he put his hand on her waist. As he moved his hand upward, she took it away.

"What's the matter?" He drew back.

"I'm saving that for marriage."

He felt the breath go out of him. "That might be a long ways away for me."

She smiled with her chin raised again. "Then that's how long you'll have to wait. We don't put the cart before the horse."

"How about kissing?"

"That's all right, if you don't go too far." She held her lips to be kissed again, but only for an instant. "I have to go now. I don't want to get into trouble."

"You don't want to lose your job, that's for sure."

"I don't want to go back to the country. I'm not afraid to work, but I've had enough of chicken feathers and dead sheep."

Alden watched her figure as she made a quick return to her work. He could not imagine setting up house at his age, but she had said a couple of things that didn't sound bad.

In no hurry to barge out into the world again, Alden led his horse down the alleyway before he mounted up. He decided to ride down the main street a couple of blocks before going home, so he turned right and then right again. Halfway down the block, he saw a familiar figure sitting on a bench in the shade of the canopy of the barbershop. Alden waved, and Cash McGinley waved back.

"Evenin', Alden. Where you headed?"

"Home. It's about that time." Alden stopped Badger.

"In a hurry?" Cash looked cool and relaxed in a billowing white shirt and brown corduroy trousers.

"Not that much." Alden climbed down from his horse, gathered his reins, and walked toward his friend. "What's new?"

"Not much. How about you?"

Alden hesitated for a second. "Maybe you heard that Grant left home." Closer now, he could see Cash's prominent forehead, pale blue eyes, and small chin.

Cash touched his wavy blond hair as if to smooth it into place. "I think I might have heard something. Did he have a fight with your old man?"

"They had some words. Nothing physical. But they're both pretty hardheaded."

Cash stretched his upper lip over his teeth. "Well that's too bad. But there's not much you can do when they're both that way. Me, I like to do things the easy way, but sometimes people won't let you." Cash gave a quick smile, and it disappeared. "As for your brother, I suppose it leaves more for you to do."

Alden dragged his cuff across his brow. "It does."

"Grant took his horse, I imagine."

"Yes, he did. No one thought to argue about that."

"That's what I need, is a horse to ride. To get out and look for work."

"Oh?" Alden had not known Cash to work any more than he had to. Maybe his parents were pushing him.

"That's right. I thought that if Grant didn't take one, you might have an extra."

"We've got two. That's all we've got left on the place. Of course, the old man doesn't ride much anymore. I don't think he's been on a horse for over a year."

Cash raised his eyebrows. "Well, if it turns out to be an extra horse, it might be what I need."

"I could mention it."

"I don't know how much it's worth, but I know you'd be fair. I'd be afraid to buy one from a horse trader. And I could pay you as soon as I started making wages."

"Uh-huh. Well, I can ask."

"Been to see Claudette?"

The abruptness caught Alden off guard. "Well, I have, actually. Just a little while ago. I don't get much of a chance. Work during the day, then take care of things at home. The old man's not doing well, you know."

"I heard that. Feel sorry on his part. Not to mention it keeps you from seein' the girls."

Alden smiled. "I do what I can. But I don't know about girls. They want you to show up more, and then they keep you at an arm's distance."

"Isn't that the truth?" When Alden didn't answer, Cash said, "They want you to do things their way, and if you always let 'em, there you are. They'll always be tellin' you what to do."

Alden wondered how Cash had so much more knowledge about girls, or at least let on that he did. Maybe Cash was repeating things he had heard. Alden pursed his lips and said, "I guess I'd better be moving along. I've got everything to do at home."

Cash looked past Alden as he said, "Well, it's too bad your brother run off on you like that, but you'll get through it."

Alden frowned. "I don't feel as if he ran off on me."

"Oh, I didn't mean it that way." Cash smiled. "You'll do fine."

"I'll do what I have to, anyway."

"You'll do swell. You're smart. Always readin' a book, at least when we were in school."

Alden felt that Cash was buttering him up after having made the comment about Grant. "I try to learn, one way or another."

"Me, too. 'Course, when I was in school, I was always tryin' to figure a way of lookin' at the girls without gettin' caught by the teacher. So a book was a good thing to pretend to be lookin' at. But it seemed like I was always gettin' caught anyway. Then when you have to sit in the corner, you can't see anything."

Alden pulled his reins through his hand. "You can learn from that, too."

Cash gave a short laugh. "What I needed to learn was how not to get caught. But don't let me keep you. I know you need to get goin'."

"I do. And I'll keep in mind what you said about needing a horse."

"Oh, that. I almost forgot."

Alden led Badger into the street, set his reins, and mounted up. "So long, Cash. I'll see you later."

Cash smiled. "You bet, Alden. Good luck with everything."

Hiram Clare breathed with his mouth open as he stood next to Alden at the stove. Alden felt an annoyance at having his father so close with his stale breath and his unwashed presence.

"I'll be glad when we finish off this hunk of bacon," said the old man. "I don't like to complain about grub, but I could go for something else."

"I'll see what I can get tomorrow. I'm sure there's some fresh beef in the butcher shop."

"By God, I never thought I'd have to buy beef from someone else, but that's where we are."

"I saw a nice antelope today. Maybe I could go for one of those when the weather cools down."

"There's better meat, but it's all right if you fry it in bacon grease." The old man breathed in and out. "Sometimes I don't care if I eat, and sometimes I get hungry as hell. Today I wanted eggs. I could have eaten half a dozen."

"I don't know if I can buy any of those tomorrow, but I

imagine I can find some meat."

"Get me a bottle if you can, too."

Alden tensed.

"I haven't had a nip all day. Savin' my last little bit for after supper." The old man breathed. "It's about all I've got left to enjoy."

Alden poked at the potatoes in the skillet. Grant, being older, had always bought the bottle.

The old man spoke. "You don't bring much news from town."

"I saw Cash McGinley today."

"Oh, him. What does he have to say?"

"Not much. Says he's lookin' for work."

"I wonder how hard he looks."

"I don't know. He says he needs a horse, so I imagine he wants to do more than walk up and down the main street."

"Do you know of any kind of work he's done?" The old man lifted a piece of fried bacon off the plate and took a bite.

"He painted a couple of buildings downtown. And I think he's pretty good with machines."

"You mean mowin' machines and threshers?"

"Well, that, too, I suppose. But I know he's worked on a couple of sewing machines, and he told me awhile back that when he was in Laramie City, he saw how they worked on automobiles."

"Then what's he need a horse for?" The old man poked the rest of the piece of bacon into his mouth.

"To get around. First off, to look for a situation. After that, maybe he needs one to travel around and look at people's machinery." After a few seconds, Alden added, "He asked if we had a horse for sale."

The old man made a smacking sound with his lips. "You mean Baldy."

Alden pictured the sorrel horse with the wide white spot

from his forehead to his nose. "Yes," he said.

"I don't think much of it."

"It would be one less animal to feed through the winter."

The old man's eyelids raised, showing more of the yellowed whites. "A horse can forage for himself."

"But we talked about leasing our section for someone to turn in a bunch of cows."

"So we did. One horse won't make much of a difference."

"It's one less animal we could charge for. Anyone would see it that way. As for how much he eats, you yourself have said that a horse will starve out a cow."

"And it's true. But I still don't think much of it. I suppose he wants to take it now and pay later."

"I think he would like to."

The old man shook his head. "I'd say no. We're not that broke yet."

"We've sold every cow we had, and we're still behind on the mortgage."

"You think I don't know that, and me not bein' able to work? I'll tell you, your brother didn't help us a bit when he pulled out."

Alden ran his hand along Badger's neck, petting him. In the shadows of the alleyway in early evening, the horse's flecked grey coat and dark ears, mane, and tail had a softer tone than in broad daylight. Alden felt a closeness with Badger. He was a good horse, never restless and never uncooperative. He was gentle and loyal. Grant could turn his back on the family, the old man could whine and complain, Claudette could make her demands, but Badger was always true. Alden could feel it, and his love for his horse welled up in him. He fought back tears as he hoped he would never have to sell Badger. Alden realized that someday, far from now, he might not be able to ride a horse anymore—not unlike his father—but he hoped that was a long ways off. Meanwhile, Badger was the one thing Alden could come back to and depend on.

The back door of the hotel opened, and Alden's heartbeat quickened as he took in the blond hair, white apron, and shapely figure. Claudette walked toward him in quick steps that caused a movement in her hips, and Alden could not help watching.

She spoke in a low voice. "It's been almost a week. I thought you didn't care anymore."

"Five days. And I've been here every evening."

"I've told you. This is the busiest time for me." She expelled a breath. "But I'm here now, even if it's for just a few minutes." She held up her face as he moved toward her, but after a brief kiss, she withdrew.

Alden had a sad feeling he could not identify as he met her eyes.

"So what have you been doing?" she asked.

"The same as always. Work all day, go home, do chores, cook supper, look after my father."

"Is he getting worse?"

Alden did not enjoy her bluntness, but she was not impolite as much as just getting to the point. "Not that I notice," he said. "But he doesn't do much. I don't know how much firewood he could carry in if he had to."

"Well, I'm glad my folks aren't that old, and they've got others at home to help out. That's farmers for you. Lots of kids. Back in Indiana, everyone's got ten kids. Or they have that many, and they don't all live. But they've got enough to do all the work and then take care of the folks when they're old."

"That's the theory," said Alden. "Sometimes it's just more mouths to feed, and when it comes to inheritance, there's not much to go around. Kids always want to leave the farm. That's how the cities fill up."

"If the parents have enough, they can spare a few. You work growin' up, and you've done your share for the family."

"Like you?"

"You could say that. I've worked on the farm, and now I've worked in town. You know I don't want to go back."

"I know." He wanted to touch her, but he was afraid she would take his hand away.

She shifted where she stood. The motion of her body set off a wave within him, but he held himself still.

"You look worried," she said.

"I've always got something to worry about."

"That's what's wrong with you." She moved forward.

He met her in a kiss, fuller this time. His hand found her hip, her waist, her snug rib cage beneath her bosom.

She drew away without having to fend off his hand. "See?" she said. "Isn't that better than getting all tied up about things?"

He blinked his eyes. "Of course it is. But it only lasts so long, and then I have to go back to everything else."

"It's because you let things be that way."

"It's the way things are."

"They could be different."

He could feel his heart beating, but he knew he needed to keep his own ground. "I couldn't do it," he said. "I'm not old enough."

"You're seventeen, and I'm sixteen. That's old enough for a lot of people. If you're old enough to work for a living, you're old enough to run your own life."

"It's not age all by itself," he said. "It's my circumstances. I've got my old man to look after. I can't go off and have a life for myself while I have that responsibility. My brother can, but I can't. Especially since he left it all to me."

She tipped her head and held her brown eyes steady on him. "Are you your father's keeper, then?"

He hesitated. "I guess in a way I am."

She took a full breath and stood with her shoulders straight. "Well, what do you want, anyway?"

He almost blurted out that he wanted to do what was right, but he thought it would sound flat or even make her laugh. He searched for words. "I'm trying to decide what are the right things to do and what are the things to avoid."

"That doesn't sound very definite."

"I know. That's why I stumbled in saying it."

"Well, I want things to happen."

"I understand that."

"I want to get out of the ruts I'm in. I don't want to plant potatoes and feed animals, and I don't want to be a kitchen girl, much less a biscuit-shooter."

"I know."

"You know everything, but you don't want to do anything."

"That's not true. I just don't want to do anything the way you want to, all at once."

"Then don't. There's plenty of fellas that do."

Alden blinked twice as he felt his heart sink. He imagined a single file of cowpunchers, each on his horse with a rope tied to his saddle, each one looking for a girl to dig the spuds and pluck the chickens. "I won't hold it against you that you said that."

"You'd better not. And don't think I'm just talking."

"I wouldn't want you to go away angry."

She seemed to have settled down, as if she had seen that she wasn't going to have things her way, at least for the present. "Oh, no," she said, "it wouldn't serve any purpose."

"People need friends."

She laughed. "I thought you were going to try to sweet-talk me. But you're right. We can be friends." She gave him her hand before she turned and walked away. Her motion still kept his attention.

Evening was drawing in as Alden walked his horse along the alley. He felt a sadness, as if he had lost something, but he sensed it was not something he was meant to have.

When he reached the open street, as he was wrapping the reins around Badger's neck, he gave the horse a hug. He took off his hat and laid his head against Badger's cheek.

"You and me," he said.

He put on his hat, set his reins, and stepped up into the saddle. He squared his shoulders and took a deep breath. Maybe he wasn't as free as an antelope, but he could make his own decisions.

Chapter Three

The town herd was grazing north of Castle Butte and inching its way westward. Now at the end of the summer, the grass had turned brown everywhere. It broke at the touch of a hoof, and particles rose in the air. The sagebrush had ripened, as had the weeds wherever the ground had been broken. Russian thistle, as it was called, grew stirrup high and dark green, waiting for the cold weather and the wind to turn the plants into tumbleweeds. The air lay heavy on the land, causing Alden to drowse as Badger poked along.

Alden shook his head to stay awake, then dismounted and yawned. He took a few deep breaths as he walked, leading his horse. The heat of the earth rose through his boot soles. Red ants labored on a hill of granules. Large grey beetles crawled across bare spots of ground. A grasshopper, as long and round as Alden's little finger, started up, clacking as it spread its yellow wings. In a couple of weeks, or a month at most, the grasshoppers would be dead and the ants would be keeping underground. Alden recalled the fable of the grasshopper and the ant. It was like the parable of the prodigal son, except that the grasshopper died from cold and hunger.

Alden raised his head to survey the land around him. He hadn't seen an antelope for several days. From late spring to midsummer, it seemed as if he had seen antelope every day or so—sometimes a lone buck, sometimes a doe and a fawn or a mixed bunch. Wherever they were now, he imagined they were feeding up for the weather to come.

Anyone who lived off the land had better be thinking ahead as well. Despite the illusion of constant hot weather, the days were getting shorter, and the nights were cooler. This was the time of year when a cold, wet spell could roll in with sodden grey clouds. First frost would fall not long afterwards.

Alden imagined the ranches and homesteads and miscellaneous dwellings, scattered across the landscape, each a stronghold in its own way against the elements. As his thoughts traveled, he recalled the girl in the ranch wagon, the girl with dark hair and dark eyes, who had looked back at him. He wondered if she lived anywhere in the area, and if she did, what kind of place she lived on. Judging from the looks of the man who was old enough to be her father, and from the way they were both dressed, Alden imagined they were homesteaders. On the other hand, the man in the dark hat could be a hired man, and the girl might even work for wages as well. Whatever the case, Alden did not think they came from a large cattle operation of their own or from any other station much higher than his.

Alden brought his thoughts back to the moment as he counted the herd. He stopped in his steps, and he counted again. He still had only eighteen, one short. He flipped his reins around Badger's neck, mounted up, and rode to higher ground. From there he took a careful count, using his hand, fin-like, to separate the animals as he scanned and counted. He still came up short, and by now he could tell that Julia Redwine's Jersey cow was the one missing.

He chastised himself for having let his attention wander. Now he was going to have to leave the main herd by itself as he searched for the stray. As he turned Badger in the direction the herd had come from, he tried to be sure of the last place where he had had the right count.

Over one rise and another, he recognized how different a place could look when a person approached it from the opposite direction. As he reconfigured where he was and where he had been, all he saw was browning grass—not a cow, not an antelope, not a jackrabbit.

On a hunch, he headed southeast, the direction the cow had taken on an earlier occasion. As a general rule, cattle did not travel very fast, but a fugitive cow with a dim sense of purpose could cover a mile in ten minutes or less. Alden figured that if he did not find this one within twenty minutes, he would have to begin riding in a wide arc.

He rode for the high points, pausing at the top of one hill after another. From time to time he looked back to be sure of his bearings. He located Castle Butte each time and resumed his search.

At long last he found the cow, knee-deep in green grass in a small draw. Riding down the slope, Alden saw no water, only damp earth pocked and scarred by animal hooves. The Jersey cow stood in the middle of the seep, her feet buried in mud, so the grass was not as tall as it had looked like at first.

Gnats and flies buzzed in the humid air as Alden circled the green spot. He untied his rope from the saddle, swung out a short length, and slapped the cow on the hip. To his surprise, after a few swats, he rousted her out of the damp area and headed her in the direction of the herd.

As the shady brown cow lumbered along, Alden wondered how it could have found its way to the little oasis a couple of miles away. He knew that cattle could smell water, as in a body such as a river or a reservoir. He had heard that horses could smell dampness in a patch of ground and would resist going in and getting bogged down. But he wondered if a cow such as this one could have been drawn by such a faint trace over a distance of two or three miles. He thought it improbable, and he also doubted that such an animal would have a higher level of intelligence or intuition. It was more likely, he thought, that the cow remembered the place from one or more earlier visits and headed back to it when the whim struck her.

At day's end, Alden chose not to mention the cow's escapade to its owner. Julia did not ask, and Alden did not volunteer the information. He thought it would make him look less responsible, or even less grown-up, than he wanted to be.

Having delivered all the animals to town and not seeing any of them wandering about, Alden pointed Badger toward the way station. Once there, he dismounted, loosened the cinch, and let the horse drink. The evening was quiet, as usual, with only the sound of a barking dog drifting on the air.

The front door of the station opened, and a man walked out. Alden recognized the Professor in his dark-brown, short-brimmed hat, brown wool vest, and white shirt. As operator of the stage station and telegraph office, he was something of a public figure. He was also Alden's boss, as he managed the business of the town herd by collecting from the townsfolk and paying Alden. Today being the fifteenth of September, Alden was glad to see his paymaster.

The Professor drew a gold watch from his vest pocket, looked at it, and put it away. The thin gold chain caught the light of the slipping sun, as did the wire rims on the Professor's glasses. He smiled as he came to a stop and poised his hand on his hip.

"And how's the herdsman today?" he asked.

"Well enough."

"No complaints?"

"None to mention."

The Professor smiled again. He had grey eyes, a touch of silver at his temple, and flecks of silver in his trimmed brown beard. "I'm sure you know that it's payday today."

"I think it crossed my mind."

"So many other things to think of," said the Professor. "Good job for a philosopher. You can think of a thousand different things in a day, and you still get to come back to civilization. Not like some of these sheepherders, who go crazy out on their own for so long."

"I try to mind my work, but I do get the chance to think from time to time."

"As long as you come back every day and bring the animals." The Professor tipped his head to each side as he smiled. "Very well. And here are the shekels." He held up his hand with his thumb and fingers pointed downward, and he dropped three five-dollar gold pieces into Alden's palm. "Or ducats, if you prefer."

"All the same," said Alden. He slipped the coins into his pocket. "We're not that far from a change in weather, don't you think?"

The Professor scratched the underside of his beard. "I wouldn't be surprised." After a pause, he added, "I hope everything is all right out your way."

"Oh, it is. My father's not so well, you know."

"So I've heard. You're a good lad for doing your part."

"Thanks." Alden hesitated and said, "If you know of any work that comes up when this season is over, I'd appreciate it."

"I'll remember that." The Professor winked. "I'm the town's repository of things to be known and remembered."

"If I ever have a question, I'll know who to ask." On reflection, Alden said, "Or whom."

"That's good," said the Professor, almost laughing. "Not afraid of the correct pronoun."

Hiram Clare was eating tomatoes out of a can when Alden opened the front door and walked in. The old man was wearing a coat and had a blanket covering his lap and legs.

"I got hungry as hell," he said. "I didn't know when you were going to get home."

"It's just about the same time as usual. Sun goes down sooner. That's the difference."

"I was cold all day. Fact is, I took cold in the night, and I never warmed up."

"You could have lit a fire."

"Tryin' to save. Lightin' the lamp was bad enough, but I needed some light so I could open this can. Besides, I'm not gonna sit in the dark forever."

"No need that you should."

The old man tipped up the can and made a sucking sound as he took in the last of the contents. He lowered the can, wiped his mouth with his coat sleeve, and smacked his lips. "I'll tell you what I think," he said. "I want to sleep in the front room, now that the weather's getting colder."

"The days are still warm. It was hot today. But the temperature goes down at night."

"That's what I mean. I tell you, I got cold last night. And it wasn't the first time. This part of the house is always warmer, especially as we get into winter."

"We're not into fall yet. But I can move your bed out into this room if you want. The cookstove heats up the front part of the house in the morning. You won't have to get out of bed until you feel like it."

"That's what I was talkin' about. I don't know how long I'm gonna last, but I don't want to die of the cold if I can help it."

"I can move the bed after supper."

"Why don't you move it now? That way, it won't be so cold at bedtime. It's always a bad beginning, crawling into a cold bed."

Alden took a breath, told himself to be patient, and went

about the work of moving his father's bed frame and bedding.

During supper, Alden observed his father. The old man's yellowed eyes were not looking any better, and his face had the same irregular blemishes. He hadn't shaved in a couple of weeks, so his whiskers were beginning to make a beard, although it was not trimmed around the edges. The old man's mouth seemed to hang open more than before, and his whole demeanor had an expression of fatigue.

"Feeling any warmer?"

"Well, the stove helps, and the grub helps as well. But you eat cold food like I did earlier, and it takes a while to stoke your boiler."

"How about the firewater?"

"Not as much as people say, unless I've had something to eat."

Alden did not speak for a couple of minutes. When he finished his plate of food, he said, "I've given some more thought to Cash McGinley and what he said about needing a horse."

"You have."

"Yes."

"And you think you want to sell my horse?"

"I'm not thinking of it in those terms."

"I'll tell you. You limit yourself to one horse, and something happens to him, you're in a hell of a fix. And there's times you need two."

"If we keep him in at all, we've got to feed him something. And if we turn him out—well, we talked about that. We want to lease this land for winter pasture."

"I wouldn't sell a horse to someone unless he had cash in hand. But I'm not goin' to be around forever, and I suppose you've got to learn for yourself." The old man took a bite of biscuit.

"Even if it takes me a month to squeeze the money out of

him, at least it's something. It'll help. I don't know how we'll get through the winter otherwise."

Crumbs flew out as the father's voice rose. "You think I don't know that? And no thanks to your brother. Sure, sell the horse. Sell every damn thing you can. Work all my life to try to put a few things together, and end up like a dog in the dark." The old man's lower lip trembled. "You don't know what it's like. You're young. You don't think about anyone but yourself."

"I go out and work every day."

"I know you do. I didn't mean that."

Alden had to admit to himself that he didn't know what it was like to be in the old man's condition.

Alden found Cash McGinley in the front room of his parents' house, trying on a buckskin shirt with fringes on the sleeves and blue and red beads on the cuffs.

"Did you find a job with the Wild West show?"

"No. I traded for this. An old cap-and-ball pistol that was lyin' around in a drawer doin' nothing." He held up his right arm to admire the beadwork.

"Is that part of your wardrobe for looking for work?"

"It could be." Cash smiled. "You can't go lookin' like a beggar unless you want to work like one. What are you doing?"

"I brought by that horse in case you'd like to look at him."

Cash's eyebrows went up. "Oh, sure. I don't have much time, but I can look at him."

"He's outside here."

"You bet." Cash lifted a hand to smooth his hair. "You go first. I'm right behind you."

Alden turned and walked through the open door. Cash followed. Down the steps, Alden paused where he had tied Baldy to the hitching rail. "There he is."

Cash tipped his head back and forth. "Pretty much as I

remember him."

"Would you like to ride him?"

"I don't have time right now. I trust you. He hasn't thrown anyone, has he?"

"Oh, no. But let me lead him around, at least, so you can see he's not lame."

"Oh, sure." Cash gave a quick nod. "Go ahead."

Alden untied the horse, led him into the street, and took him through a couple of figure-eights.

"Looks good," said Cash. "I don't see anything wrong with him."

Alden waited.

"What I mean is, I think he'll do fine for me."

After a few seconds of silence, Alden said, "We haven't talked about the price."

"I guess you're right." Cash tossed a glance at the horse. "How much do you want for him?"

"Thirty dollars, cash in hand."

The young man's lips tightened across his teeth as the corners of his mouth tucked back. "Like I said before, I wouldn't be able to pay for him until I found work. Of course, that's what I need him for."

Alden had to force himself to stick with what he had told himself to say. "My old man says it's thirty now or forty later, and if we don't get paid in two months, I'll have to take the horse back."

Cash rubbed his nose. "Seems a little steep, and I don't know if I can come up with forty dollars in two months."

"You could sell your shirt."

"If only I could." He patted Alden on the shoulder. "It's all right with me. Let's put him in the stable in back."

★ ★ ★ ★ ★

Alden turned up the collar on his denim jacket. Clouds had been piling up in the west all day, and a cold wind blew out of the northwest. He had been expecting a cold spell, and here it was, on the twenty-fifth of September. He could smell moisture in the air, feel the chill on its way. The country was in for either a cold rain or an early wet snow.

Animals could sense the weather coming. He knew it, and he could see it now. The town herd had been jumpy all day, and he had kept a close watch on all the stock. He counted them again. Nineteen. All present.

Alden maneuvered Badger so he could keep his back to the wind. On a cloudy day such as this, he found it harder to guess the time, but from the hints of shadow from the taller hills and from Castle Butte in the distance, he guessed it was time to start heading home.

He rode back and forth along the western edge of the grazing animals, slapping the loose end of his rope on his boot and calling, "Yep! Yep! Let's get movin'." Princess, the cream-colored mule, frisked one way and another, and some of the calves wanted to frolic, but after several minutes, Alden had all nineteen head moving toward town. The bell on the lead cow tinkled as all the hooves scuffed and thudded.

He tried to take each day as it came and not get ahead of himself, but he knew the season was approaching its end. He had been told from the beginning that his work would last until snow covered the ground. After that, people would sell some of the animals, butcher some, and feed the rest through the winter. Owners might turn their stock out during a spell of open weather, but they would do so on their own. The town herd would be dispersed until spring.

No work meant no money. He would be free to gather firewood and to hunt for meat, but the mortgage payments would stack up. Money brought in through leasing or through any day labor he could find would disappear in the purchase of basics such as potatoes, beans, flour, bacon, and canned goods—and the old man's bottle. Alden could not see a way around this last item unless the old man gave up all the way, and even that was not a solution to the larger problem.

Alden shook his head. Expense, his father's health, debt—it was more than he wanted to think about, but he had to. At the same time, he needed to focus on the day at hand. He had a herd of animals to convey to their owners, and after that he had his tasks at home.

Once in town, he was pleased that all the animals went to their pens without any trouble. As he turned Badger onto the main street, he put his work behind him for another day.

As a matter of habit, he rode down the alleyway behind the Landmark Hotel. He had ridden that way every day for two weeks, since the last time he spoke with Claudette, and the door was always closed.

Today the door was open. The sounds of human voices and clanging kitchenware floated out. Alden stopped his horse and dismounted, feeling a mixture of worry and hope.

Before long, a man stepped outside. Bare-headed and wearing a white shirt and apron, he walked toward Alden. He had a determined expression on his face.

Alden drew himself up straight and took in a breath. Unsure of what to say, he came out with "Yes, sir?"

The man had a heavy face and thinning hair. He wrinkled his nose and said, "Look here, kid. We don't need you moonin' around back here. Don't bother."

"I just—"

"Your little bird isn't here anymore. She flew away."

Alden's heart sank. "Where to?"

"That's not for me to say."

"Did she go home?"

The man pronounced each syllable slow and flat. "I don't think so."

Alden's head went dizzy, and he heard himself speak. "Did she get married?"

"I already told you. It's not for me to say."

"Thanks," said Alden, for lack of another word. "Sorry for the bother."

"It's all right. You don't know any better. But there's no reason for you to come back."

Alden's head was still swimming as he led his horse to the end of the alley and into the street. He patted Badger on the cheek and said, "I guess we ask the Professor."

He mounted up and rode the two blocks to the station. After watering his horse, he walked to the door, taking reluctant steps. As he was about to knock, the door opened, and the Professor stood smiling with the grey afternoon light glinting on his eyeglasses.

"Yessir, my young friend."

Alden made himself speak. "Mr. Baker, I'm sorry to bother you, but the last time we talked, you said I could ask you if I had a question about anything going on in town."

The Professor's teeth showed as he smiled. "I don't know if I said that, but you can try me out. The worst I can say is—well, I don't know what the worst would be until I heard the question."

Alden took in a deep breath. His mouth was dry. He couldn't make himself ask about Claudette, so he thought of something else. "I was wondering if you know a man I saw in town a while back. He came in on a wagon with his daughter, it looked like. He was dark-haired, and he wore a black hat and a black neckerchief."

"Friendly sort?"

"Not that I noticed."

"Then I think it might be Jack Wilcox. Dark-haired, scowling sort of fella. Comes into town about once a month, sometimes has his daughter along." The Professor gave Alden a close look. "Are you interested in her?"

Alden shrugged.

"Well, I don't know her name, if that's what you want."

"No, not really."

The Professor drew his brows together. "Did this fellow give you some trouble?"

"No. I saw them on the street one day, that was all."

"Hmm." The Professor continued to study Alden. "It's your business and not mine, but it seems there's more to it than what you've said. You seem worked up about something."

Alden shook his head. "Nah."

"Look, kid. If there's something troubling you, don't be afraid to ask. You don't have to carry things around by yourself. Is it about something else?"

"I don't know."

"I'm not good at guessing."

Alden let a few seconds drag by. "Well, yes, it's something else."

The Professor's face relaxed, and he gave a wry smile. "It's just you and me, my friend. It won't go any further."

Alden swallowed, moistened his lips, and cleared his throat. "It's about a girl, but not these Wilcox people."

"Oh. Well, go ahead."

"I don't know if you know who she is, but her name is Claudette Cushing. Blond girl. Works in the hotel kitchen, or did. They said she left."

The Professor's eyebrows went up. "Oh, yes. I think I heard something. Were you kind of sweet on her?"

"I can't say she was my girl, and the last time I talked to her didn't end well, but—"

"I don't want to say anything unkind about her, anyway. But you asked." The Professor paused. "You say she left, and I imagine you'd like to know how or where."

"That's right. The man at the hotel made it seem as if she . . . eloped with someone."

"From what I heard, I think it might be something like that."

Alden had a leaden feeling in the pit of his stomach. "I don't have any claim on her. Not at all. But I'd like to know what happened."

"It could be worse," said the Professor. "According to what I heard, she ran off with a young fellow, and they set up housekeeping in a little bungalow out on the Fisher place. Do you know where that is?"

"Yes, I do. It's a few miles south of town. Not so far out as I live, and a ways west."

"That's right."

"Well, it's good to know where she is. Do you know the name of the fellow she went with?" Alden braced himself.

"McGinley is what I heard. Young fellow about your age. I've seen him up and down the street."

"I know him."

"I thought you might. You look a little pale. But I'll tell you. You'll get over this. And if you live a normal life, it won't be the worst thing that ever happens to you."

Alden's mouth was still dry, but he found words. "Thanks. It's just not a good time for me to have to hear something like this. I feel like I've been kept in the dark and punched in the stomach."

The Professor patted him on the shoulder. "There's never a good time, and believe me, I know how it feels."

★ ★ ★ ★ ★

Alden slumped in the saddle, watching the town herd at the end of a cold, drizzly day. He had a slicker to keep off most of the rain, but he and his saddle had been wet around the edges by midmorning, and conditions did not improve. Now, in late afternoon, his hat and his boots were soaked.

The herd animals had become slow and obstinate, but he rounded them up and headed them back to town. His last stop of the day, as usual, was Julia Redwine's place. Julia appeared in a hooded oilskin raincoat that was bulky enough to have been her husband's.

As she swung the gate closed, she signaled for Alden to wait. He relaxed in the saddle, watching the rain drizzle down Badger's mane.

Julia flicked beads of moisture from the hood of her coat and smiled. She said, "I have a package for you to leave off for Claudette, if you would. I understand she's living in a place that's on your way home."

"Not exactly, but I can go by that way if I need to."

"She'll appreciate it, I'm sure. It's not a big package, or very heavy, but it has things that a woman needs."

Alden looked from one side to another, uncertain about what to say.

"She sent the order in with Cash, but he won't be back until tomorrow. He said I could ask you."

"I see."

Julia's voice rose in a cheerful tone. "That's all right. You don't have to. It's out of your way, and the weather's miserable."

"I'll do it."

Julia's smile shone from within the rain-beaded hood. "Oh, that's a dear. I know she'll appreciate it, and I do, too."

★ ★ ★ ★ ★

The bungalow, as the Professor called it, was a low-slung, drab-looking building with weathered lumber soaking up the rain on the north and west sides. Alden had ridden past it before, but this was the first time he had a reason to stop. The house was bigger than a homesteader's shanty, but it had gone the way of many, as the original owners had sold out and gone elsewhere. The outfit that bought it went into insolvency, so it belonged to the bank now. Alden had heard it was situated in a bad place for snowdrifts in the winter and snakes in the summer, but people rented it from time to time.

As he approached the house, he saw that the corral was empty. He imagined Cash in his buckskin shirt, riding Baldy, in a sunny place where he didn't need a hat.

Alden came to a stop and called in a loud voice. "Anyone home?"

The front door opened, and Claudette stepped out. She waved as if they were good friends who saw each other once a week. Alden waved back, then rode up to the front porch and dismounted.

He took the package, wrapped in paper and tied in string, out from under his slicker. He said, "Julia Redwine asked me to deliver this."

"Oh, good," said Claudette, reaching out her hands. "I was hoping you would. Cash won't be back for a couple of days."

"Looking for work?"

"Yes, and it's not a good time for it. And somebody's got to bring in some money. They won't let me work at the hotel now, of course."

Given how unreserved she was, Alden did not hold back. He asked, "Are you married?"

Claudette wagged her eyebrows. "Kind of."

"What do your folks think of that?"

She shrugged. "They don't want to have anything to do with me. Not for the time being, anyway."

Alden could not grasp how she could be so casual about something that he saw as being so enormous. He said, "Is this what you wanted?"

"Nothing's perfect. But I don't have anyone telling me what to do." She waved her hand at the house. "This is where we start. We'll work up from here. In another year, we'll have our own place. Wait and see."

Alden did not say anything.

"You're not sore, are you?" she asked.

"Oh, no. I've got no reason to be."

"That's what I told Cash."

Alden fidgeted. He did not feel that he was doing any good at the moment, or that he even belonged here. After all, her husband, or whatever he was, was away, and here was Alden, who not so long ago was trying to spoon with this girl. "I should be going," he said. "I've got a ways to go, and things to do when I get there."

She said nothing.

"Well," he said, "I hope you're happy. Or on your way there."

"I'm fine. I'd worry about you, though. You've got so much weighing on you. I can see it."

"Don't worry about me. Look out for yourself. Winter's not far away."

"I'll be fine. This'll be better than that cold room at the hotel, as far as that goes."

Bundling, Alden thought. Again he did not have anything to say.

"Thanks for dropping off the package," she said.

"Glad to."

"Don't be afraid to come by again. We're friends, and you never know when one person can help out another."

"Sure. And if you need something, just ask. I'll help if I can."

"You should have been a banker."

"Thanks, I guess. I'll see you later." He led his horse away, checked his cinch, and mounted up. He turned and saw her waving as she had done when he rode in, so he returned the gesture. As he rode out of the yard, he pondered her comment. He did not think he had the natural makings for a banker. Maybe she meant that if he was a banker, she would have favors to ask. That was probably it—not much of a compliment, but practical from her view.

Alden stirred the mixture of meat and gravy so that it would not stick to the iron skillet. Around the cookstove, small wisps of steam rose from the trousers, jacket, and wool socks he had hung on the backs of chairs.

His father spoke from his seat at the table nearby. "The longer you cook it, the better it is. Gravy doesn't taste so much like flour, and the meat isn't so tough." When Alden did not answer, his father continued. "I hope you don't get another chunk of beef like that. The stuff you cooked last night was so tough I could hardly eat it with the teeth I've got left."

"I know. That's why I'm cooking the last of it in gravy."

"At least there's meat. I can remember times when all I had was bacon grease and flour. Times are hard now. Well, they were harder then, workin' any job I could find, and two little kids to feed."

Alden took a steady breath. He had heard it all before, more than once, but it was better for everyone if he didn't say anything.

The old man shivered in his coat. "It got cold today, and this is just the beginning."

"We usually have a spell of mild weather after this first squall."

"Yeah. Indian summer. More like Indian giver. Time of false hope."

Alden stirred the gravy. As far as he knew, his father had never met an Indian.

The old man rested his hands on the table as he began to roll a cigarette. "If you stop in town tomorrow, I could use another bottle. I'll be ready for a new one at about this time tomorrow."

"I stop in town every day."

"I know that. I meant to buy supplies."

"I need to pick up some other things. I can buy a bottle." Alden watched as his father rolled the cigarette. For the first time, he imagined his father standing at the stove and watching his two little kids eat. "Do you need tobacco?" he asked.

"I'm not out, but I could use some of that, too, now that you mention it."

Light rain was pattering on the roof, and the interior of the house was dark. Alden opened the door and looked out to see what he could expect for the day. The predawn sky was dark with a heavy overcast of clouds. He could smell the moisture and feel the chill. He closed the door, hoping his father would not complain about the draft.

He lit a lamp and held it up to see that his father was covered all right. The glow of the lamplight fell on the old man's tousled grey hair and untrimmed beard. The old man's mouth was open, but he did not seem to be breathing.

Alden moved closer and bent over, laying his hand on the blanket where it covered his father's shoulder. The body was still and unmoving to the touch. Alden laid the back of his finger on his father's cheek, and he felt the cold firmness of death.

CHAPTER FOUR

Snow was piling up on the hitching rails along the street as Alden paced the length of town. The restlessness in his legs would not let him sit in one place until he had his business resolved. He kept an eye on the bank, waiting for the sight of Mr. Newton Dorrance returning from lunch.

Alden reached the west end of town where the buildings ended. He lingered, gazing out toward the landscape, where visibility ended in about half a mile. He imagined Castle Butte with undisturbed snow gathering on the cedars, pines, and rocks. He cast his thoughts in the other direction, where snow would be accumulating on the house and barn and corrals of the Clare homestead. A pang of sorrow moved through him, causing him to fix his eyes on the buildings of town. He turned and resumed his walk, heading in the direction from which he had come.

Across the street and down a couple of blocks, a man in a dark homburg hat and a matching overcoat approached the entrance of the bank. He was not taking hurried steps, but he was not on a leisurely stroll. He walked with repose, pushed the door open without a flourish, and walked in.

Alden crossed the street, making himself not hurry. He needed to give Mr. Dorrance time to settle in behind his desk, and he needed to prepare himself to measure his words rather than blurt out everything he had in mind.

Inside the bank, he took off his hat and coat and let his senses adjust. The interior was shadowy in comparison with the white-ness outdoors. He had seen the inside of the bank very few times, and even though the most recent occasion had been an hour earlier, he had to take in anew the features of the counter, the teller window, the desks, the vault, and the office where Mr. Dorrance sat at a desk beyond an open door. The teller, a man with wire-rimmed spectacles and slicked-back hair, greeted Alden with one clipped syllable.

"Yes?"

Alden had his first sentence rehearsed. "I've come back to see if I could speak with Mr. Dorrance."

"I'll see if he's available. Your name?"

"Alden Clare."

The clerk moved away, his heels sounding on the wooden floor. He stood in the doorway to the office and spoke in a low voice. After several seconds of waiting for an answer, he returned to the counter, reached under to click a latch, and swung a hinged panel inward.

"Mr. Dorrance can see you now," he said.

Alden walked to the doorway and stood with his hat and coat in hand. Lamplight illuminated the desk where the banker, with his shiny bald head bent down, was writing on a lined sheet of paper. The scratching of the tip of the pen carried across the small, quiet room.

Dorrance looked up. The lamplight fell on his round, gold-rimmed glasses, his ruddy cheeks, and his bushy white mustache. He set his pen in the inkwell and stood up. He was slender and below average in height, wearing a neat grey suit with a gold watch chain drooping from his vest. "Come in," he said.

He reached across the desk, shook Alden's hand, and told him to sit down. When they were both seated, he spoke again.

"I'm sorry for the death of your father."

57

After a month of such condolences, Alden had learned to say, "Thank you."

"I was sorry to have to issue the order to quit the premises, also," said the banker. "But there was no other way. It was the next step in the process."

"I didn't know we were being foreclosed on."

"Your father was informed. It was his mortgage. He owed more than the land was worth, and he had gone well over a year without making a payment. When an account is that far in arrears, we have no other recourse."

"It came as a surprise to me."

"Well, I must say, we gave him ample notice. Everything went according to procedure, and we have records of it all."

"I don't need to see them. I believe it." Alden had an indistinct memory of Grant delivering envelopes to their father and of the old man burning papers from time to time.

"As his heir, you would have a right to. But we don't just hand things over the counter. An attorney for the estate could ask for a review. You have a brother, don't you?"

"Yes, I do. He left a while back, and I don't know how to get in touch with him."

The banker made an automatic half-smile with no other expressions to accompany it. "I'll leave it to you. But to make it easy on you, and perhaps to save you unnecessary expense, I will say that there's not much chance of reversing the process at this point."

"I think I understand that. Or maybe I should say, I am beginning to understand it."

Dorrance sat back in his chair, with his hands folded on his stomach, and nodded. Behind him, his dark herringbone wool overcoat with a black fur collar hung on a standing coatrack.

Alden cleared his throat. He could feel his heartbeat picking up, so he made an effort to steady himself. He said, "What I would like to ask today, sir, is what the chances are for me to get it back."

The banker sat up straight. "Well, you would have to buy it, just like anyone else. Like I've already said, there's not an option at this point to make up delinquent payments or to negotiate a new plan."

"I understand that. What I would like to know is whether I could have the chance to buy it back at some time."

"Start all over again."

"Well, yes."

The banker raised his eyebrows. "It's a noble idea, boy, but it's not very practical. If the bank were to sell a piece of property such as this one, to a person or party who did not have cash in hand, the bank would have to be able to determine that the party had resources or the prospect of resources to make the payments. You understand that. We can't lend money on the basis of good intentions."

"Yes. I intend to work and to save money. At some point I would like to know how much money I would have to put down."

"All of that would depend upon the price at the time and the buyer's prospects for income."

"But it's something we could talk about, later."

"By all means."

"Very well. Thank you, sir." Alden stood up.

Mr. Dorrance rose from his chair, leaned forward, and offered his hand as before. "And best of luck to you, young man. I know it's not easy."

Alden walked out of the office in something of a daze. He observed the teller's clipped, greying mustache and pointed nose, he heard the click of the latch as the half-door closed behind him, and he smelled the fumes of tobacco smoke on a portly man who pushed past him in a wave of cold air as the door opened.

Outside, a light snow was falling like before. The world was quiet. His father was in the cold ground. His brother was off seeing bright lights and bigger towns. The homestead was abandoned, and Alden could not go there. He did not have a job. All he had was his dear horse Badger, and a bit of money he had saved from his wages. He took a deep breath and swallowed against the tightness in his throat.

For the first time, he put it into words for himself. His family had fallen apart, and he did not have a home. He was free in a way he never would have wanted. But he could work, and he would rise in this world by working. Someday he would have a piece of land to call his own, and in good time, he would think about a family.

Alden rode southwest from the town of Morse. The snow clouds had passed over, and a fragile autumn warmth had spread across the rangeland. According to what others said, and what he had observed for himself, this was a good time to hunt, as the animals came out after weathering a storm. With time all his own, Alden had decided to hunt deer; and having slept for several nights in the livery stable, he was not afraid to camp out in chilly weather. If he did not find a deer within a couple of days, he could go back to sleeping in the hay and could ride out in the daytime to look for antelope. It was all a good plan as he reviewed it, and he felt the most optimistic he had felt since before his father died. The sun was shining, and Badger was stepping along at a brisk pace. The troubles of life fell away for the time being, and Alden was free in a good way.

The tinkling song of a meadowlark carried on the clear air. If any grasshoppers had survived the snow, they were not yet warmed up enough to fly. Alden associated the grasshoppers with heat, dust, dryness, and brittle grass. At the moment, the world was gentler—damp in places from the melted snow, with the dust settled. Badger's footfalls had a softer sound than they did a few days earlier, and the dry prairie grass did not break and then rise in particles. Even the pliant grass would make hunting better.

He rode southeast with the sun warming his shoulder. He pictured the place he was headed toward, the breaks, as being at the apex of a long isosceles triangle, with Castle Butte and the town of Morse making the other two points. The breaks made for good deer country, thanks to the many canyons and crevices where deer found cover. They holed up in the middle part of the day, coming out to graze in the morning and in the late afternoon, as well as at night during a full moon. Alden recalled the moon he had noted the night before, and he was glad that it was only at a quarter.

Except for the prospect of a few deer, the breaks were not regarded as desirable country, as they did not offer good grazing for livestock and had rough, jagged inlets where a cow could hide out and where a man had to go in on foot to roust her. Although cattle seemed like clumsy, lumbering beasts, Alden had learned that they could navigate trails through dense thickets, under low branches, on steep hillsides, and through narrow mazes. The breaks had all of these features, as well as snakes. With the recent snow, Alden figured that the snakes at least had gone into dormancy.

Beyond the breaks to the west, the country ran to more hardscrabble range, where a few homesteaders held out. South of the breaks, the rangeland was poor also. Alden had a mental picture of the country—brittle, alkaline soil with sparse grass— and he did not know of anyone who lived there. In contrast, the rough country of the breaks was an oasis, with occasional tiny springs and strips of green grass.

With the breaks in view, Alden adjusted his course so that he would strike them at the east end. They ran east and west, rising like a row of low-lying buttes, with most of the crevices facing north. Alden planned to hunt on foot, moving along to the mouth of one little canyon after another.

He found a likely spot for a camp. He picketed Badger to a stout bush, stowed his saddle and bedroll and canvas sheets in the shade, and drew out his rifle. It was a Winchester '73, one of the few valuable items he had salvaged out of the foreclosure. He had hunted with it before, and now it was his.

He started out on foot, carrying the rifle in front of him with his finger outside the trigger guard. From time to time he raised the rifle to his shoulder and practiced lining up on an object. The motions became smoother as his hands guided the rifle, found the balance, and snugged the butt against his shoulder.

On one such maneuver, he was startled to find himself pointing the rifle in the direction of another person. A bearded man in a brown hat and a brown-and-yellow flannel shirt had stepped around the protruding wall of a crevice. He made a large wave with his arm.

Alden lowered his rifle and called out. "Sorry. I didn't know there was anyone else around."

As the man walked forward, he said, "Neither did I." He was carrying a rifle and wore a hunting knife on his belt.

They covered the fifty feet between them and stopped when they were a couple of yards apart. The other man was about thirty years old and husky. Alden let him speak first.

"Looks like you're hunting, too."

"I am. I just started. Have you had any luck?"

"None with deer. My other luck's bad."

"In what way?"

"My horses ran off."

"That's too bad. How many are there?"

"Two. I got up this morning, and they were gone. I thought I had 'em picketed better than that. So I been lookin' for them and keepin' an eye out for deer at the same time." The man's eyes traveled over Alden. "Where you from?"

"I'm from around here. And yourself?"

"Shawnee. Work in a blacksmith shop there."

Alden nodded. He placed the town, about a day's ride to the north and a little west.

"Name's Bill. Bill Smith." The man held out a large hand, and the two of them shook.

"My name's Alden Clare." After a few seconds of silence, he said, "I hope you find your horses. And get a deer, of course."

"So do I."

"I think these breaks are big enough that we don't have to crowd one another. Have you seen anyone else?"

"Not here." Bill Smith gave Alden another short look of appraisal. "I suppose you know most of the people hereabouts."

"North and east of here, yes. As far as over that way, to the west, I can't say that I do."

"Well, north and east is the way my horses seem to be headed."

Alden felt a sense of obligation settling upon him. "I could help you if you'd like."

"Nah. I know you want to hunt. I don't want to keep you from that."

"It wouldn't be that much trouble. I've got a horse, and he could be a big help in catching loose horses. I've had to chase 'em on foot, and I know they can string you out all day, keeping a quarter of a mile away from you."

"That's for sure. But I don't like to be a bother."

"No bother. I'll help you find your horses, and then we'll come back, go our separate ways, and we'll each get our deer."

"As far as that goes, I want to kill two. Make it worth my while. But that's beside the point."

"You need your horses no matter what, so let's see if we can find them."

"Well, all right. I appreciate it."

They left their rifles wrapped in Alden's canvas sheets, then struck off across the rangeland to the northeast. Bill insisted on walking and letting Alden ride. He walked at a fast pace, keeping an eye on the ground as well as surveying the landscape. Though the day was warm and drying, the ground had been damp enough overnight that Bill found hoofprints at sporadic intervals, though the prints were so faint that Alden could see only a few of them from where he sat in the saddle.

After about an hour, Bill said, "I kinda got a hunch that these horses might have had some help."

"You think so?"

"Yep. They're not wanderin' enough for stray horses. I hate to admit it, but I'm not that good of a tracker. I can't say with certainty whether two or three horses made these tracks. On a dirt trail I could tell you, but not here."

Alden took a sweep of the surrounding country. "I haven't heard of horse thieves out in the open like this. Everyone has heard of the secret trails through the Rawhide Buttes and the Laramie Range, but not around here. On the other hand, I suppose anything is possible."

"I'm not jumpin' to any conclusions. Just seems like there might be someone in on it."

As they moved on, Alden tried to maintain his sense of bearing. At one point, the town of Morse lay almost due north, and the Clare homestead, which was no longer his home, lay almost due east. Then the angles changed as Alden and Bill continued to the northeast.

Alden caught an occasional glance of Bill Smith on foot, forging along. Alden knew that all of the country was new to Bill, while it was new to him only in the sense that he was seeing it from a different direction than usual. As he adjusted his sense of where he was, he realized they were headed in the direction of the Fisher place. By Alden's calculation, they would come up somewhere near the backyard or back door of Claudette and Cash's bungalow.

Alden had a strange sense of being an accomplice. Cash may have ridden out on Baldy, and as he had not yet paid for the horse, Alden was still, in some sense, the owner. Furthermore, with Cash and Claudette being his friends of sorts and Bill Smith being a stranger, Alden felt as if he would be seen as being on the side of the local residents.

By Alden's estimate, he had ridden seven or eight miles, with Bill Smith hoofing alongside. As they topped a rise and the bungalow came into view a quarter of a mile away, Bill spoke.

"Do you know who lives here?"

"I believe I do."

"It might be best if you introduce me, then. I'm pretty sure those are my horses in his corral."

Alden felt a tightness in his stomach. "I can do that," he said. "Let's circle around and go in the front way."

One of the horses began to nicker as Alden rode into the yard with Bill Smith at his side. When Badger nickered in return, Alden realized that Badger was greeting his old friend Baldy.

The door opened, and Claudette appeared. She was wearing a grey dress such as she would have worn on the farm. She shaded her eyes with her hand and waited as Alden and Bill came to a stop some twenty feet from the house. Her eyes went back and forth, then came to a rest on Alden. "What can I do for you?" she said.

"Is Cash at home?"

"He's still sleeping. He was up late."

Alden resisted making a comment out of place. He dismounted and stepped forward. "This is Bill Smith. He's from

Shawnee, and he's down here hunting. His two horses disappeared, and we tracked them to here. To tell the truth, Bill tracked them."

Bill took off his hat, and his full head of brown hair reflected the sun. "I'm Bill," he said. "Bill Smith. And those are my horses that someone put in your corral."

Claudette gave a polite smile. "I don't know anything about it. You'll have to talk to Cash." She turned and stepped into the house.

Alden and Bill exchanged a glance as Bill put on his hat.

After several minutes of standing in the sun and feeling anxious, Alden flinched at the opening of the door. Cash stepped out, squinting into the daylight. He was bare-headed, and for once, his hair was not brushed into place. He shaded his eyes and said, "Good mornin', Alden. What can I do for you?"

"Cash, this is Bill Smith. Bill, this is Cash McGinley." After a couple of seconds, Alden said, "As I told Claudette, Bill's from Shawnee. He came down this way to hunt deer, and his horses got away on him. We followed 'em to here."

Cash looked at Bill.

"Those are my horses," Bill said. "In your corral." When Cash did not answer, Bill added, "I would guess you put 'em there."

Cash, still squinting, said, "They just drifted in here. Woke me up in the middle of the night. Hungry, I'd guess. Maybe wantin' the company of another horse."

"They're mine."

"I don't know that yet. But whoever they belong to, I did him a favor by penning 'em up."

Alden's eyes widened on their own. He thought Cash was a bit brazen.

Bill said, "I won't argue about the details of your story. But I want my horses back, along with their halters and picket ropes."

"Some men would offer proof of ownership."

"I've got a bill of sale at home, but I don't carry it around with me. Those are two sorrel horses, no brands. One has a narrow blaze, and the other has a white sock on the right hind foot." Bill took a breath. "And the halters are both horsehair, hackamore style, with five-eighths-inch picket ropes made of hemp."

Cash raised his eyebrows. "You sound like you're accusing me. I'd think the real owner would appreciate what I did, maybe even offer me a little reward."

"I want my horses back, period. I don't want to have to go to the law, but I will if—"

Bill did not finish his sentence as Claudette emerged from the house and stood next to Cash.

She said, "If they're his horses, why don't you just let him have them?"

Cash scowled. "I didn't say I wouldn't." Shifting his gaze toward Bill, he said, "Take 'em. For all the thanks I get for keepin' 'em from being taken out of the country."

"I want my ropes and halters."

Cash spoke to Alden. "They're in the shed. You can help him. I'm going inside. I haven't had a cup of coffee yet."

As Cash stepped into the house, Alden saw that he was in stocking feet. Claudette moved aside to let him pass. She lingered for a moment to smile at Alden and then at Bill.

"There's no harm done," she said. "And I'm glad you've got your horses back."

"Thanks, ma'am." Bill took off his hat again, held it against his chest, and made a slight bow.

Claudette smiled again and made a graceful turn as she went back into the house.

Within a few minutes, Bill had both horses ready to go. "I'll ride this one," he said, patting the sorrel with the white blaze. "I can ride him bareback easy enough and lead the other."

As they rode out of the yard, Bill looked back at the horse he was leading. From Alden's perspective, it seemed as if Bill cast a glance at the front door as well. But no one appeared.

At the top of the first hill, Alden drew rein and let Bill catch up. "Sorry for the inconvenience," Alden said.

"No need for you to be sorry. You didn't do anything except help. I wouldn't give much for that other fella, though. How'd he end up with her, anyway?"

"That's more than I know."

"Well, I got my horses back. That's what matters."

They returned to Alden's camp by midafternoon, and finding nothing out of order, they agreed to hunt in their separate ways, each beginning at one end of the breaks and working toward the middle.

On his hunt, Alden saw a doe and then a doe with a fawn. He had it in mind to try for a buck, so he let the others alone. As the afternoon moved into evening and the sun slipped behind the mountains in the west, he heard two rifle shots.

"Bill Smith," he said to himself.

Alden began the morning hunt from the same place as before. Now he had the sun at his back instead of in his face, and the shadows would fall in the opposite direction from the way they fell the day before in the little canyons. He reminded himself that deer tended to graze in the sunlight in the morning and in the shadows in the afternoon, at least at this time of the year. With these conditions, he looked forward to a new hunt.

After a couple of hours of stalking, and having seen nothing larger than a coyote, he stopped for a rest at the edge of a silt-stone canyon wall.

Within a few minutes, the world began to fill in around him. He heard the buzz of a fly and the whine of a small cloud of gnats. A breeze sighed across the prairie grass out on his right. A small rock squirrel appeared on a ledge of the facing wall. Overhead, a hawk soared, its dark feathers forming an outline for the light-colored feathers of its underbody. Beyond the hawk, a pure blue sky gave the illusion that all days would be like this one.

A faint thud came to him, not only a sound on the air but a feeling in the earth. It came from an animal larger than a deer, maybe a cow, maybe a horse, maybe more than one. He laid his rifle across his lap.

The sound came closer. Alden stood up and was ready to fade into the shadows of the ravine. He heard the snuffle of a horse, and Bill Smith rode into view. Bill was riding the sorrel with the blaze, saddled with a bundle tied on back. The second horse carried a pair of canvas packs with two sets of forked-horn antlers tied on top.

"Whoa," said Bill, reining to a stop.

"Looks like you got your deer."

"I did."

"Do you have them both in those two bundles?"

"Yep. I don't bother with heads, hides, lower legs, or rib cages."

"All meat."

"That's right."

"I heard two shots along about evening," Alden said.

"That was them." Bill smiled. "I thought I'd come by and let you know. I'm headed home now."

"Good for you. I hope you have a safe trip."

"And good luck to you. See you again some time."

"So long, Bill."

Alden watched as Bill and the two horses rode away to the

north, in the direction of Castle Butte and beyond. Alone again, Alden resumed his hunt.

Luck favored him an hour later when he saw the tail end of a deer disappear into a narrow canyon. Backing up to the canyon he had just passed, he turned left and took the softest steps possible to work his way in.

A hundred yards into the ravine, he followed a cow path up the side of the ridge. Near the top, he crept one short step at a time until his sight cleared the crest. A little higher, he could see down into the next canyon. At first he saw only a doe, motionless in the shadows, pointed toward the opening. Shifting his gaze, he saw a second doe, standing ahead of the first one. Scanning again, he made out a third deer. His pulse jumped when he saw the dull shine of antlers.

He ducked out of view, levered a shell into the chamber, and crawled into position. He relocated the deer and made sure of the one he wanted. After taking a breath to steady himself, he lined up the sights behind the deer's shoulder, waited for the right second in time, and pulled the trigger.

The buck lurched, and the two does leaped away. A few yards out, they turned and watched as the buck thrashed and went still. As Alden stood up, the two does spun and fled.

Alden picked his way down the narrow canyon and stood over the deer he had killed. The buck was sleek and muscled, not large and not small. Each side of the antlers had three points, a long tine and a forked one. It would have been a good deer to take home to his father and brother, but his life was in a different stage now. He was on his own. This was his deer, evidence that he could manage for himself.

He observed the buck for another moment. He could not imagine eating a whole deer before the meat spoiled, but he could imagine sharing it. As he stood with the rifle in his hands and the deer at his feet, he felt the responsibility of not letting the meat go to waste and the freedom of choosing how to go about it.

Leading Badger with his camp outfit and his deer meat tied on snug, Alden walked into the front yard of the bungalow in the middle of the afternoon. Baldy nickered from the corral, and Badger answered. A minute later, the front door opened and Cash stepped out. He was dressed in the same clothes as the day before, and he was wearing boots.

He ran his hand over his hair, raised his chin, and said, "What have you got there?"

"Deer meat."

"Oh. I thought maybe it was your pal."

"No, he killed his two deer and went home."

"I hope he stays there."

Alden did not answer.

"I didn't like the way he came in here. And to tell you the truth, I didn't like the way you took sides with him."

Alden hesitated. If anything, he had helped Cash stay out of trouble. "I don't believe I took sides. Like Claudette said, there was no harm done. And he's gone now. I came by to give you two some deer meat if you want it."

Claudette appeared in the doorway and stepped out into the sunlight. She was wearing a light blue dress, and her blond hair was tied in a ribbon of the same blue color. Cash looked at her as if he was seeing something different or unexpected.

Her voice had a cheerful note. "Say, Alden, what have you got there?"

"A deer. I thought I'd share some with you two, if you want any."

"Of course," she said. "Every little bit helps."

"I'll have to untie my load, then. I've got the animal skinned and quartered, but I packed the meat with my camp gear on top to keep the sun off."

"Cash'll help you. Won't you, Cash?"

"Yeah. I need to do something first."

He walked into the house, and Alden figured he was going out back.

"I'll get started on my own," Alden said.

Claudette's voice was still cheerful. "Can I help?"

"You can hold the horse."

Alden untied his bedding and set it aside, then untied the two canvas bundles and set them on the ground. "What do you think of a hindquarter?" he asked.

"Whatever you want to give us."

"A hindquarter is good meat, and it's not so much that it would spoil on you."

"Oh, I'll make good use of it."

By the time Cash returned, Alden had his load packed again and tied down. After a brief round of thanks and goodbyes, he led Badger out of the yard. When he looked back, the front door had closed. Cash and Claudette had gone into their bungalow.

Dusk was settling on the main street as Alden trudged into town. Julia Redwine had not closed up her dry goods store, so Alden tied his horse in front and went in.

Julia was pleasant as always. "Good evening, Alden. What brings you here?"

Alden thought she looked tired, and as on earlier occasions, he was impressed by her ability to keep up her energy at the end of a long day. "I had some luck hunting deer," he said, "and I have more than I need for myself. I thought I'd ask if you'd like some."

"Why, that's very generous of you. You don't have to, you know."

Alden shrugged. "I've got plenty, and I don't want it to go to waste. A hindquarter isn't too much, is it?"

"Of a deer? No. Especially with the weather cooling down. It won't spoil."

"Good. I'll fetch it."

Outside, he untied his knots as before and set his bundles on the wooden sidewalk. He hauled out the remaining hindquarter, hefted it in his arms, and carried it into the store.

Julia led the way through the store to the living quarters in back, where he left the meat on the kitchen table. He followed her into the store again, where she stopped short at the appearance of two customers.

"Oh. Good evening," she said. "We were in back for a minute."

As Alden moved around, he caught sight of a dark-featured man in a dusty black hat. By reflex, he looked beyond the man and saw the girl with dark hair and dark eyes, dressed in a canvas jacket, a work shirt, and overalls.

Julia's voice rose. "Alden's a good boy. Or, I should say, young man. He's been out hunting, and he brought me a quarter of a deer. Very generous of him."

Alden thought she sounded self-conscious about having come out of the back of the store with him, but he had nothing to add.

"I seen his stuff all over the sidewalk," said the man in the black hat.

Julia stepped aside. "Let me introduce you. This is Alden Clare. And Alden, this is Mr. Jack Wilcox and his daughter, Bonnie."

Alden took off his hat. "Pleased to meet you both." His eyes met Bonnie's, and he wondered if she remembered him from the day on the street.

Jack Wilcox's voice cut in. "We see 'em all the time. Them

and antelope. We can get one any time we want." He turned to his daughter. "Let him by."

Bonnie stepped behind her father, and Alden had no choice but to walk past them. With his hat still in hand, he nodded to Bonnie and walked out onto the sidewalk.

As he gathered his belongings and tied them onto the saddle one more time, he kept an eye out for the dark-eyed girl in work clothes. He did not see her again, and he had no plausible reason for going into the store, so when he had his knots tied, he led his horse away into the gathering darkness.

CHAPTER FIVE

Alden found the Professor in his living quarters in the back of the way station, where lamplight showed through the window.

"Whoa!" said the Professor as he opened the door. "It's my young friend. What do you need?"

"Sorry to bother you after dark, but I went deer hunting, and I have more meat than I need for myself. I thought I'd offer you some."

"That's good of you. As long as it's not something tough, like the hocks."

"Oh, no. I'll tell you what I've got. I gave away the hindquarters, so I have the loin straps and the two shoulders."

"Any of that would be all right, although some of that shoulder meat could be tough."

"I'll be glad to give you some of the loin."

"On the other hand, I don't want to take your best cuts."

"Like I said, I have more than enough."

"Here's an idea, then. I was just about to start a fire in my cookstove. I can fry us up some of that loin. Unless you've got other engagements."

"Not at all."

"Good enough. Bring in a chunk."

The Professor sipped from a glass of whiskey as he poked the chops around in the sizzling bacon grease. "I was just thinkin' of you earlier in the day," he said.

"Oh?"

"Fella named Willis Squire, lives over east, could use a hand for a couple of days."

"That's good. I could use the work."

"He's supposed to drop in tomorrow. I told him I thought I knew of someone."

"I appreciate it. But before I jump at the offer, maybe I should know what kind of work it is."

"A good practice, but I don't think there's anything to worry about in this case. He finished his fall roundup, and his hired hands all left for the winter. Now he finds out that someone over west of here is holding three cows with his brand. He needs someone to help him bring 'em back."

"Sounds like something I could do."

"That's what I told him." Lamplight reflected on the Professor's eyeglasses as he poked again at the frying meat. "Are you sure you don't want a modicum of whiskey?"

"No, thanks," said Alden. "I haven't acquired a taste for it yet."

The Professor smiled, showing his even teeth. "No hurry. You've got the rest of your life to try out all these things."

Alden presented himself at the way station at eight o'clock the next morning. The Professor, dressed in a brown wool jacket, vest, and pants, and topped off with his dark-brown, short-brimmed hat, was sitting against the building in the sunlight and drinking a cup of coffee.

"Mr. Squire has been here and gone," he said.

Alden had a sinking feeling of disappointment. "You told me to be here at eight."

"He went to buy some horseshoe nails."

"Oh."

"He brought a packhorse, and I believe he likes to go

prepared. How did you do with your deer?"

"I gave a shoulder to Joe at the stable, and I left the rest hanging in a shady place wrapped in light canvas."

"That should be good enough. The rest of the loin you gave me won't go to waste, that's for sure. Ah. Here comes the boss now."

Alden followed the Professor's hand motion. A man on a bay horse was approaching from town, leading a brown packhorse. The man wore a tan canvas coat and a grey wool cap with a short beak, and his clean-shaven face reflected the sunlight. He raised his hand in greeting as he rode up to the station. He brought the bay to a stop, pulled the packhorse around so that the lead rope would be out of the way, and dismounted. With the reins in one hand and the rope in the other, he walked forward.

The Professor stood up. He tossed away the black residue of his coffee cup and said, "Here's the young helper I mentioned."

Alden, who had been standing all the while, nodded as the man looked him over. "I'm Alden Clare. Pleased to meet you."

The man transferred the reins in back of him to his left hand, then held out his right. "Willis Squire. And pleased to meet you. The Professor said you can fight Indians and live on snake meat."

"I wouldn't want to contradict him, but I might be a bit tamer than that."

"Do you have a horse?"

"Yes, sir, I do. It's at the stable. I can have him ready on short order."

"And a bedroll?"

"That, too."

"As you can see, I've brought a camp. I expect to spend one night out, be gone two days and a little more as we take the cows back to my place."

Alden nodded.

"What do you think of a dollar a day?"

"It's agreeable with me."

"Any questions?"

"None at the moment, sir."

"You'll do all right. We've all heard of the kid who came out West, and the old-timer told him he asked too many questions. The kid said, 'What's wrong with that?' "

The Professor spoke up. "When I was that age, I always had two questions—when do we eat, and where are the girls?"

The boss smiled. "Have things changed?"

"Only in the sense that I know better than to ask."

"Good enough," said the boss as he turned to Alden. "Go ahead and get your horse ready. I'll swing by for you in about fifteen minutes."

The first day's ride took them west and a little south. Alden saw Castle Butte on his right, on higher ground to the north. As he rode on, he formed a vague picture of the country to the south, west of the breaks, where he understood that Jack Wilcox had his place. The boss had not given any names or details, and he did not show any interest in the rangeland to the south.

They camped that evening on a small trickle of a creek. After a meal of biscuits and cold beef, the boss spoke.

"I don't know this country very well. The people from over here don't come east all that much. They tend to deal with folks along the main trail from Cheyenne and from this side of the mountains. The river's not that far from here, I don't think, and the trail follows it for quite a ways. Curves up and around to Douglas and on to Casper. I know the general layout, but I don't know the people. Sometimes when you get into a pocket of the country, people can be clannish and jealous. And, as for their practices, I don't know what to expect. Three of my cows wandered all this way, and not a calf among 'em. Not that I'm surprised. I wouldn't even expect to see the cows again, except that whoever was overseeing the fall roundup wanted to take care of all the details."

"You don't think there'll be trouble, then."

"No, not at all. I just didn't want to drop in and expect some strangers to put us up. This way, we can come and go and not impose on anyone."

When they crested a hill overlooking the Pilcher headquarters the next day, Alden thought a county fair was going on, though it was late in the year for such an event. A large, round tent was rippling in the breeze, while a multitude of camp tents and ranch wagons dotted a ten-acre flat. Close to the barn, corrals and shipping pens were crowded with horses. People meandered through the scene, some on foot and some on horseback.

A man on a buckskin horse rode out to meet the two newcomers when they reached the bottom of the hill. He had dark hair, a dark mustache, and a high-crowned cream-colored hat. He wore a light blue shirt with dark embroidery, plus a pair of grey leather gloves with dark-blue gauntlets.

"Buyers?" he asked.

"I don't follow you," said Squire.

"For the horse sale. We've got buyers, and we've got sellers. I suppose some people just come to look. Since you're not bringin' anything in, I thought you might be buyers."

"I didn't know you were having a sale."

"You bet. Lotta horses comin' off the range, plus a cavvy of almost two hundred from a trail drive. People come fifty miles or more. Gonna be bronco ridin', too, and a dance later on."

"Sorry we can't stay for it. My name is Willis Squire, and I've got a place over east between Castle Butte and Silver Springs. I received a letter from Ross Pilcher telling me he was holding three cows of mine. They've got a Six-Bar-M brand."

"Oh. Then you need to talk to Martin. Wait over there in front of the barn, and I'll send him to you."

Squire led the way, with the packhorse and Alden following. When he reached the area where people were milling on foot, he dismounted. Alden did the same. They walked through the crowd and past the pens of horses. At the barn, Squire said, "I can hold your horse if you need to take care of anything."

"Not right now."

"Stretch your legs if you want. See the sights. We'll be here for a few minutes at least."

Alden handed him the reins and set out on foot. The atmosphere was indeed like that of a fair, with rising voices, laughter, and somewhere a child crying. The aroma of roasting meat drifted on the air, and dust rose from the pens. People walked everywhere—men and women, boys and girls, little kids. They were all strangers, and they all ignored him, except for one man who was selling a saddle.

"Get this while the price is right, sonny. Get rid of your old Mother Hubbard."

Alden shook his head and moved on. He walked past an area where four or five men were squatted and kneeling, one of them poking at the ground with a stick as the others chewed and nodded.

Alden stopped. The man with the stick had a dusty black hat that registered in Alden's mind. Jack Wilcox. He had his back to Alden and was talking to the group, but half of his creased face was visible.

Alden moved on, his heart beating and his arms tingling. He doubted that Jack would leave Bonnie at home alone for a few days. Then again, maybe he did, if they had stock to tend to. Still, it was worth an effort to see if she was here. Alden picked up his pace and took a close look at every little group of people he saw.

He stopped at the sight of flowing dark hair. He was sure he recognized it, along with the canvas jacket and denim overalls. The girl had her back to him as she stood near four or five other people watching a man paint a portrait. Alden walked toward her, his heart beating in his throat. He was afraid it might not be her, terrified that if it was, he would do something wrong. But he pushed himself forward until he stood at her left elbow.

"How do you do?" he said.

She turned, and he met her dark eyes less than a yard away. Her face softened in recognition.

"I met you the other day in the dry goods store," he said.

"You were giving the lady some deer meat." Her voice was clear and pleasant, not faint.

"That's right. And I saw you one time before, on the street. You were in the wagon with your father, and you turned to look at me."

"I remember."

"Your name's Bonnie, isn't it?"

"Yes."

"Mine's Alden."

"I remembered that, too." She smiled. "I didn't expect to see you here."

"Neither did I. I came here with a man to pick up some cows. We'll be going right back."

"You're in a hurry, then."

"He doesn't want to waste time. And he's the boss."

Her eyes met his. "I remembered you from the first time on the street."

He almost melted. "And I remembered you. You can be sure of that." An urgency, almost a worry, gnawed at him. He had only a minute, and he did not want her father to walk up on them. "I'm sorry," he said. "My boss is waiting, and I've got to go." His mouth felt dry, but he made himself speak. "When can I see you again?"

She shrugged. "I don't know. I live a long ways out."

"Could I visit you?"

"I don't know. I suppose. My father doesn't like outsiders, but—"

He waited for her to finish her sentence.

Her eyes moved away, then came back. "He knows everyone has to grow up."

"I can't be afraid to try."

She looked over her shoulder, as if she, too, expected her father. Nevertheless, her voice remained steady. "Do you know where I live?"

"Not exactly, but I can find you. South of Castle Butte and west of the breaks, isn't it?"

"That's right. They call it the Hermit Flats."

He touched her hand, and their fingers clasped. He felt the current run through his upper body. He would have given anything to kiss her, but this much would have to be enough for now. "I'll see you," he said.

For the first several hours of the return trip, Alden felt as if he was in a swoon. As the sun began to slip behind the mountains, however, he gave his surroundings more attention and became aware that they still had miles to go. The shadows were lengthening even from short objects like the clumps of sagebrush. Alden felt a chill, and he flexed his upper body muscles to increase circulation.

Squire said, "It's gettin' late. That place was farther than I figured, at least in terms of how long it would take us to come back. I don't know of anywhere out here where we can put up these cows."

"Neither do I," said Alden.

"Then I suppose we plod along in the dark. I wish we had a better moon."

The town of Morse was asleep when Alden and his boss turned the three cows into the corral at the livery stable.

"I might as well sleep here, too," said Squire. "We can put up our horses, and we can go straight to my place in the morning."

Alden decided not to sleep in his usual cot in the harness room. He was dog-tired when he rolled out his blankets in the straw. Squire was smoothing out a bed for himself nearby. In a low voice, Alden said, "What do you know about the Hermit Flats?"

"Poor country, and from what I've heard, hard-grubbin' people who live there. Why do you ask?"

"I know someone who lives there."

"Oh. Was that the girl you were talking to? Don't mind what I said about 'em, then."

Alden felt his spirits sink into his bottom blanket. He felt as if half the world had seen him talking to Bonnie.

Squire made no further references to the people of Hermit Flats as he and Alden went about their work the next morning. By midday they had the cows delivered to Squire's ranch, east and north of town.

The boss dropped three silver dollars into Alden's palm. "Thanks for the help," he said. "If I need a hand again, I'll let you know. And if you're looking for work in the spring, drop by here around the tenth of May."

"I'll do that." Alden expected one more comment, about work or about the Professor, but the boss said nothing.

As Alden rode down the gradual slope that led westward

from Squire's headquarters, his thoughts soared over the town of Morse and across the big country some ten to fifteen miles. It was a long ride to be turned away by a surly father, but he would give it a try.

Alden was cleaning stalls in the livery stable when a voice behind him made him jump.

"Who's in charge here?"

Alden turned around to see a man in a brown hat and a large, flowing, turquoise-colored bandana. He wore a dark-brown fur coat, hanging open to show a black leather vest and an ivory-handled revolver.

"You'll need to talk to Joe," Alden said. As his eyes traveled over the man again, he noted a deep blue shirt with lapels and a full row of buttons, then a pair of tan leather gloves with blue and red beads on the gauntlets. At first he thought it might be the man who had ridden up at the Pilcher horse sale, but that man had dark hair and a dark mustache. This man had hair the color of dead winter grass, and his mustache was so light as not to be apparent on first glance in a shadowy stable.

"I need a place for my horse," said the man.

Alden recognized the voice at the same instant that he recognized the birdlike nose that was flattened at the tip. This was the man he had met a couple of months earlier on the range. Today he was dressed for appearances.

"I'll find him." Alden set his shovel against a stanchion and went in search of Joe.

The stable man was in the harness room, where he sat on a chair as he spliced a loop into the end of a rope.

"Customer, Joe. A man wants to leave his horse."

Joe set the rope aside and rose to his feet. "Just one horse?"

"I think so."

The two of them walked out into the open area of the stable.

The well-dressed man was swinging his arms back and forth, fanning the air with his gloved hands. He hunched his shoulders and said, "Gets cold."

"It does," said Joe. "I understand you want to board a horse."

"That's right."

"One day?"

"We'll see. I've got a few things I want to look at."

"Bring him in."

Alden went back to work with his shovel and wheelbarrow. He looked up when the stranger led the dark horse into the stable.

"Name?" said Joe.

"Cliff Worthington. Not to make a secret of things, I'm lookin' around to buy some land in this area."

"Just land?"

"I'd prefer a ranch, with buildings already on the place. But if need be, I can build."

"There's places around," said Joe. He waved his hand at the interior of the stable. "Come and go as you want. Alden sleeps in the harness room, so there's always someone here."

Worthington took a glance at Alden and returned to Joe. "That's good to know. By the way, I'm staying at the hotel."

"Have a good stay."

"Thank you. I'll do my best."

Alden rode across the quiet country, dormant now in the winter. The grasshoppers were long dead, the ants were underground, and most of the birds had gone south. Off to his right, Castle Butte rose in the cold sunlight. In a few months, hues of green would show, but for now, the colors of the landscape were dull shades of grey and tan.

Alden knew he could not rush time. But he was eager to find full-paying work so he could begin to save up. He could not bear to ride past the Clare homestead, and he knew it was abandoned. In his mind, it was waiting for him, but he kept that idea to himself. He did not want anyone to smirk at him.

He rode on toward the Hermit Flats. He did not know what he could or could not bring himself to say to Bonnie, but he had worked up the courage to see her. In less than an hour he would be knocking on her front gate, or whatever Jack Wilcox had to set off his house and yard from the rangeland.

The Wilcox dwelling faced east, with its back to the north and west, where the strongest winds and storms came from. The meager pastureland ran right up to the front step, and Alden saw no evidence of anyone having planted a tree or a garden. On the south side of the house, three people sat on chairs against the building, taking in the reflected warmth of the winter sun. A few yards from the group, a slender boy or young man was skinning an antelope suspended from the side of a wagon.

Alden dismounted from Badger and walked to within fifteen feet of the people seated. Bonnie sat nearest, then her father, and then another man who looked like a resident of this hardscrabble area.

"Good afternoon," said Alden. "I was in the neighborhood, so I thought I'd drop in. I'm Alden Clare. We met a while back in the dry goods store."

"I remember you," said Jack. He ran his tongue along the seam of his lips, then raised a cigarette and took a drag from it. "This is Paul Sherwood, my neighbor."

The other man smiled, showing a stubbled, wrinkled face with a couple of sunken spots where teeth would be missing. He had a glass in his hand, as did Jack Wilcox, and a bottle sat on the bare ground between the two of them. Sherwood waved his free hand and said, "That's my son, Sooters."

Alden glanced at the lad skinning the antelope. Closer now,

he could see that the boy was about twelve years old, thin, wearing a grey flannel shirt rolled up to his elbows. His forearms were steeped red in blood.

"Cut with your knife pointed the other way," Sherwood called. "You get too much hair on the meat."

Alden knew how the coarse, white hair could fluff off an antelope, and he could see that the boy did not have much experience. His moves were awkward, and the hair stuck to his hands and his knife as well as to the exposed animal flesh.

After a few seconds of silence, Alden let his eyes meet Bonnie's. "How do you do?"

"Fine," she said. "Nice of you to stop by."

"Not a bad day for a ride."

Jack Wilcox spoke up. "I don't mince my words. I don't care for people to come nosin' around."

"I don't snoop," said Alden.

Sherwood lowered his glass from taking a sip. "He come to see the girl."

Jack rubbed the side of his nostril. "You think I don't know that?"

Sherwood's voice had a squeaky tone as he said, "You can't stop nature."

"I don't need your help."

Sherwood fizzed a laugh. "Madge was only fifteen, and I was seventeen. Her old man would've whupped the hell out of me if he could have got his hands on me."

"Tell him to cut from the inside out."

"Sooters, cut from the inside out. Get your knife under the hide. Don't cut through from the outside. You get hair all over it."

Jack raised his cigarette and paused before taking a drag. Without looking at Alden, he said, "Who do you work for?"

Alden straightened up. "Right now, I work a few hours a day

at the livery stable. Come springtime, I've got a job lined up for a cattle outfit."

"Which one?"

Alden did not like to talk in detail about things that were not yet certain. But he felt he had to answer. "A man named Willis Squire."

Jack still did not look at Alden. "I don't know him," he said.

"I did a little work for him. He seems fair enough."

"That kid's makin' a mess out of the antelope."

"Heh," said Sherwood. "He's gotta learn some way."

Jack turned in his seat, his dark eyebrows drawn together. "Bonnie, why don't you go pump a bucket of water and give it to Sooters. Have him wash his hands and his knife, and tell him to clean off as much of the loose hair as he can."

Bonnie stood up. She was wearing a winter coat and overalls, but her hair was clean and her eyes were shining.

"I'll help if you like," said Alden.

"I can do it."

"Leave her be," said Jack. "She does it all the time."

Bonnie let her eyes meet Alden's. "Thanks for coming by," she said. "I need to go inside to get a bucket."

"I'll see you next time." Alden waited for a biting comment from Jack, something to the effect of not bothering to come back, but the father said nothing. As Bonnie walked into the house, Alden said to Sherwood, "So long. And good to meet you."

"You bet," said the neighbor. "Have a safe ride back."

Alden glanced at Jack, who tipped the ash from his cigarette and spoke to Sherwood.

"Tell him to cut off the front legs before the hide hangs down over 'em, and he forgets."

"He's doin' fine. Let him get his hands clean first."

Alden led Badger away and mounted up. As far as visits went, it could have been worse.

The south side of the main street lay in shadow all through the day in the dead of winter, so the snow and ice in the gutter stayed around for weeks. Alden kept to the sidewalk, even though it meant treading the edge where two men stood talking in front of the Mercantile. As he began to step around them, he saw that the one with his back to him was Cash McGinley, wearing a coarse grey overcoat and a fur cap that covered his blond hair. He was talking to Cliff Worthington, who wore his customary black hat, brushed clean, and a canvas drover's coat.

Alden hoped to step around them without any mention, but Cash stopped him with a cordial greeting.

"Alden! How do you do?"

Worthington tipped his head in surprise and moved aside as Alden turned to answer Cash.

"Good afternoon. Or I guess it's just noon. I'm doing well enough, I suppose. And yourself?"

"Fine. Just fine. Say, did you know that your brother's looking for you?"

"No, I didn't." Alden frowned. "I had no idea he was in town."

"He's in the café. He was going in when we were coming out."

"I'll look for him there."

"Sure. It was just a few minutes ago."

"Thanks." Alden nodded to Worthington.

The man was gazing at him with a pair of brownish-green eyes and nodded in return.

Alden walked down the sidewalk two doors and turned in. He did not recognize his brother at first, even though he was the only patron in the café and he was sitting at a table in the middle of the establishment. Grant had his head bent forward as he worked on a plate of ham and eggs, and his features were blocked out by a large, greenish-grey, broad-beaked wool cap the size of a small cushion.

"Grant?"

His brother looked up with a stolid expression, and then his light brown eyes showed recognition.

"Alden? Hey, boy. Sit down." Grant waved at the chair on the opposite side of the table.

Alden pulled out the chair and sat down, still noting the unfamiliar details about his brother—a sheepskin coat, a dark-blue flannel shirt, and striped grey wool pants.

"Are you hungry? Let me buy you a meal."

"No, thanks."

"Coffee?"

"I could drink some of that, I suppose."

Grant turned and motioned to Harry, the proprietor.

When Harry had filled a cup for Alden and had gone back to his post, Grant spoke in a somewhat challenging tone.

"I heard the old man died."

"He did. Back in October."

Grant cut into his ham steak. "Why didn't someone let me know?"

"I didn't know where you were. And besides, I didn't know if you cared."

Grant did not look up from his work. "Puh. I was in Cheyenne. Not hard to find."

"I didn't know that."

"And I heard you lost the place." Now Grant leveled his eyes on his brother.

Alden felt as if he had to defend himself. "It was foreclosed on. The old man was more than a year behind on the mortgage. I didn't know it was that bad."

"Doesn't surprise me. Did anyone get anything out of it?"

"Not to speak of. There was really nothing left to sell. I ended up with the rifle."

"There should have been another horse left. Baldy."

"I sold it to Cash McGinley."

"How much?"

"Forty dollars. But he hasn't paid me yet."

Grant snorted. "You let everyone walk all over you. Not that the place was worth much. But it was all we had."

Alden lowered his voice. "What I want to do is, I want to get it back. I'm going to work and save up—"

"I'll believe it when I see it." Grant cut off another piece of ham. "Like I say, it wasn't worth all that much, so don't feel so bad about it."

Alden recalled Grant's offhand comment, the night he left, that he might come back with enough money to pay off the whole works. He wondered if his brother remembered.

Grant spoke again. "But I don't like to see people like Cash McGinley get the best of you. I never cared that much for him, but he was your friend. Then he turns around and takes advantage of you when you don't have a pot to piss in."

"I sold him the horse before the old man died, so we wouldn't have to feed it through the winter."

"Was that before or after he took your girl?"

Alden flinched. "She wasn't my girl. I didn't have any claim on her."

Grant shrugged. "That doesn't mean he should have her." He put a scrap of egg on top of a piece of ham and shoveled it in. After a few seconds he said, "I suppose it doesn't matter. I hear they're going to have a baby."

Alden flinched and tried not to show it. "I don't know. I haven't seen her for a couple of months."

"Well, don't pay it any mind."

"You seem to have found out quite a bit in a short while."

"A fella doesn't even have to ask. People pour it out."

"I suppose so."

"And yourself? I heard you were working for your keep at the livery stable."

"Mine and Badger's. And I've got a job lined up for the spring."

"Good for you. I don't want to have to worry about you."

Alden felt a twinge of resentment, what with his brother leaving him alone and coming back when he felt like it, but he realized from the tone that Grant meant it. "I can take care of myself," he said.

"I know you can. But if you get in a pinch, don't be afraid to ask for help."

"Thanks. Do you plan on staying around for a while?"

"There's not much goin' on anywhere else."

"You must have found some kind of good work."

"Yeah, but nothin' lasts forever. Things dry up in the winter. Money lasts longer here."

"Do you have a place to stay?"

"Oh, I've got friends. And I'm not stuck here. I can come and go as I please. Are you sure you don't want something to eat?"

"No, thanks. I need to get back to work."

CHAPTER SIX

Alden stood next to the dark horse's hip as he pulled the steel comb through the tangled tail. After a winter on the range, some horses were unruly, but this one was calm. Nevertheless, Alden knew enough to stand to one side and to keep one hand on the horse whenever possible. Through the winter months in the livery stable, he had worked around quite a few horses belonging to other men, and now he was starting over with a string of horses fresh off the range. Squire had assigned eight horses to each hired hand, and it was up to that hand to be able to brush, comb, curry, saddle, and ride all the horses in his string. Alden knew that one horse could give as much trouble as the rest of them together, and he also knew that a horse that was gentle all the way through saddling could still pitch a storm as soon as the rider swung his leg over the saddle. He was yet to find that out about any of the horses in his string, for he had not ridden any of them yet.

After he had combed the mane and tail, he brushed the horse. This one, like several of the others, had not shed all of his winter coat, so the old hair lifted off like thatch. Tufts of hair from the different horses—white, reddish brown, black—lay on the ground. It stuck to his boots, his trousers, his shirt, and even his face.

Alden brushed the dark horse a second time, taking off more of the dull, shedding hair and bringing out the shiny coat beneath. He knew he would not take it all off the first day anyway. Working with horses took patience and repetition, and he would work with all of those in his string several times over.

He put away the dark horse and roped out the last one in his group, a pale-colored animal somewhere between a dull white and the winter coat of a palomino. It had narrow shoulders, and its ribs were showing. As Alden slipped a rope halter onto the horse's head, he noticed that the animal had shed all its old hair except for a few wisps behind the shoulders and along the jaw. Alden took off the neck rope and was about to tie the halter rope to the hitching rail when the horse jerked back.

With the rope around the rail, the animal first gave a short pull. Then it jerked again, yanking the rope from Alden's hand. Alden stood free and turned to keep his eye on the horse. The pale animal had set its rear hooves as it gave the abrupt, forceful pull backward. Losing resistance, it now reared on its hind legs and pawed the air with its front feet. Even though the horse was not deep-chested, it loomed like a large beast, its dark eyes glaring, its mouth open, and its belly showing. It went over backward and fell on its side, hitting the earth with a grunt and kicking to regain control. It scrambled to its feet, cut away to the left, and bolted for open ground, trailing the halter rope off to one side.

Alden stood watching, pondering how he was going to retrieve the horse. He still had his work rope in his hand, so he began coiling it. He heard steps and turned to see the boss approaching.

"That's the way it goes," said Squire. "Everyone's got to have at least one like that in his string. I can't give all the knotheads to one man."

Alden kept his eye on the pale horse, which had stopped about a hundred yards away and was looking back. "What's this one's name? Devil Joe?"

"They call him Buttermilk."

"Fits him, with that sickly white color."

"Fella who rode him last year and gave him that name was from Texas. He said that down there, if you go into a place and ask to buy milk, the storekeeper is likely to say, 'Ya'll want sweet milk or buttermilk?' "

"That fits, too. Not very sweet."

"Give him a few minutes to cool down. Saddle one of your other horses to go get him."

At the dinner table, the other two hired hands recalled the story about buttermilk and sweet milk. One of them, Jesse Burns, told of an outfit where he had worked.

"We cut the cards every day to see who had to milk the cow. None of us liked that job."

"That's nothin'," said Ben Roscoe. "One time all of our horses ran off except one. We had him penned up in an extra-strong corral because he was an outlaw. There was a storm comin'—that's why the others run off—and one fella had a broken leg. The rest of us had to draw straws to see who was goin' to ride this mean horse and go get help."

Squire said, "I imagine someone made it. You're here to tell the tale."

"Boy named Billy Mayfield drew the short straw. Horse bucked him off about thirty feet out of the gate. We set out after it on foot, three of us, and after we walked a couple of miles, we went over a hill and found the rest of our horses."

Jesse said, "Did he get his saddle back?"

"Oh, yeah. The outlaw made it back to the main ranch, and he was waitin' for us when we got there."

"And the fella with the broken leg?"

"Never rode another horse. Died in a train car."

"Accident?"

"For him. He was tryin' to help rob it. Ridin' as a passenger."

"That's too bad," said Jesse.

Ben shrugged. "Everyone gets a chance. It's a matter of what you do with it. I think he thought he got dealt some bad luck when he broke his leg and he thought he deserved something in return. But then he made his luck worse all by himself."

Squire said, "It's too bad, all right. I agree that everyone gets a chance, but I don't know if everyone gets the same chance. I can say, like I do, that I worked hard, saved my money, and got my own start. I did it on the square. I've got my own section now, and access to grazing. I could go broke at any time if a bad winter wiped me out or if the rustlers hit me hard, but for right now I'm doing all right." He paused for a second and went on. "Each one of you fellas works hard, too. But next week at this same table, or at some other table right now, there could be a fella not all that different from the rest of us, but he's got something in him that ruins his chances. I've seen it, and I'm sure you've all seen it, too. You can say they do it to themselves, but you also wonder if it could have been any other way."

"Do you think they're fated?" asked Alden.

"I don't know. But I think if a person does well, and he sees someone else who doesn't, there's only so much credit he should give himself, and only so much discredit he should give the other fella. Life comes to an end for every one of us, and many's the time it comes early for the fella who doesn't do well. But that's enough for my sermon, and no criticism intended to anyone."

Ben's voice had a cheerful tone. "None taken. As the sayin' goes, praise the Lord and pass the potatoes."

The Professor turned in his chair at the telegraph desk as Alden walked into the station with Ben and Jesse.

"What, ho!" said the Professor. "Looks like two kings and an ace kicker. What are you lads up to today?"

Ben said, "We got a day off before roundup starts. Thought we'd come into town and take care of a few things."

"Like buying some perfumed bath soap?"

"Got a good supply of that. Me 'n' Jess, we thought we'd ask you to write some letters for us."

"How many?"

"Just one each. Regular stuff. A letter to home, tellin' the folks that everything's fine. Ready to go out in a couple of days when the wagon rolls."

The Professor nodded to Ben and then Jesse. "Letter for each one?"

"Sure," said Jesse. "Same thing Ben said. All's well. Expect to be out for a month to six weeks."

Ben said, "Sign 'em for us is fine. You can address 'em, too, can't you?"

"Same addresses as last year?"

"Nothing's changed."

"I can do it. I've got the addresses in the drawer." The Professor smiled. "No letters for girls?"

"Not yet," said Ben. "We need to get some new ones to write to."

"If you could order the paper," Jesse added.

Alden's eyes opened. He had heard of men writing to women whose information they found in a matrimonial paper, but this was the first he had seen of the process.

"I can do it. We should have some letters in return by the time you boys come back from roundup." The Professor turned to Alden. "Anything I can do for you?"

"Not at the moment. I think I can manage for myself. But thanks."

"Like your namesake in the poem?"

Alden frowned. "I don't follow you."

"Why don't you speak for yourself, John?"

"Oh, yes. John Alden and Miles Standish, and the girl named Priscilla. I wasn't thinking of that."

South of Castle Butte, the grassland rolled away in waves of green, but vegetation became sparser as Alden approached the Hermit Flats. The grass grew in small clumps, with intermittent patches of bare earth and crumbly rock. A jackrabbit sprang up from out of nowhere and ran a zigzag path to the west.

Alden held to his southwesterly course and caught his first sight of the Wilcox place at a little after noon. He slowed Badger to a walk for the last half-mile. As he dismounted, he looked for movement in the yard. After a moment, he saw Bonnie's head and shoulders on the other side of a stock pen. He waved, and she had a bucket in her hand as she waved back.

He waited for her to finish her task and walk to the house. As she came into full view, he saw that she had a bucket in each hand. She put both bucket handles in one hand and brushed a wisp of hair from her face. She was wearing a light blue cotton work shirt and a pair of denim trousers, but her clothes did not hide the shape of a young woman.

"Hello, stranger," she said.

From her easy tone, he guessed that her father was not at home. "Good afternoon," he said. "Doing chores?"

"We've got a cow and a calf penned up, and I have to water them at least twice a day." She stopped a few feet away and set down the buckets.

"I had a day off, so I came out here as soon as I could."

"Nice weather for it. Where are you working?"

"For the man I mentioned before, Willis Squire. He has a place out on the other side of town, just before you go over the hill to Silver Springs."

Her dark eyes met his. "How do you like it?"

"Just fine. I'm learning more about horses, and I'm making

more than I've ever made on a job. Not much more, but some."

"That's good."

"How about yourself?"

She gave a slight smile as she shrugged. "There's always work. It's not as hard this time of year, but there's more of it. I don't mind it, though. I know you have to work if you want to get somewhere."

Alden glanced around. "And your father?"

"He's over at Sherwood's."

"Do they trade work?"

"Sometimes. Right now, I think they're palavering. That's what Mr. Sherwood calls it when they put their heads together."

Alden's eyebrows tightened. "Are they planning something?"

"I don't know how much they're planning, but I think they're talking about what they can do about some trouble we've been having."

"Trouble?"

"Yes. There's a group of three or four riders who keep coming by, and they're telling my father and Paul Sherwood to keep their animals off the public land."

"They can't do that."

"Well, they're doing it."

"Who are they? Do you know who they work for?"

"I don't know who they work for or even who they are. My father says he doesn't, either. Sometimes there's three, and sometimes there's four. I've seen only one of them before, and I don't know his name."

"What does he look like?"

"Oh, he's not very old. Maybe eighteen, twenty at the most. He's not the leader. Just the only one I've seen before, loafing around town. He's blond-haired and doesn't wear a hat."

"Does he ride a sorrel horse with a wide white blaze, what they call a bald-face?"

Her eyes quickened. "Why, yes. Do you know him?"

"I might. He's been kind of a friend of mine, but not much of late." Alden had a familiar feeling of complicity, and he wondered if this was the work for which Cash needed a horse.

"What's his name?"

"If it's who I think it is—but I shouldn't say. I don't want to name someone if it's not him."

"I understand. It's a good thought. If I find out his name, either first or last, I'll let you know."

Alden smiled. "Are you going to write me?"

Her face tensed. "I don't know of an easy way to send a letter from here."

"You mean you don't think it would arrive."

"Well, yes. Or if it did, it would have been read through, maybe more than once."

"How will you tell me, then?"

Her face had a matter-of-fact expression, and her voice was clear and steady. "The next time I see you."

"Oh."

"But if I did know of a way I could send a letter to you, how would I direct it?"

Alden reflected. "You could send it to me, in care of Mr. Cameron Baker. He's the one they call the Professor. He runs the stage station and telegraph office."

"I think I know where that is."

"On the east edge of town. And he's a trustworthy man, at least in my view." Alden's thoughts came back to the moment. "I'm sorry to know that someone's giving you trouble. No idea of who these fellows work for?"

She shook her head. "None at all."

"I sure don't have an idea. I don't know of any big outfits close by that would want to push around some—" He hesitated, not wanting to use the word "nesters."

"Little people," she said. "People who don't have much. My father says he thinks they're trying to draw him into a fight, and he says he can't figure a reason except they want to try to take this place."

"I don't know why."

"That's what he says. There's better land to be had for the taking."

Alden had a fleeting image of the place his family had lost. "Well," he said, "I'll keep my eyes and ears open, but I'm quite a ways away." His eyes met hers again. "I'm going to work with the roundup crew. I'll be gone for more than a month, maybe six weeks."

"That's good to know. I won't worry if I don't hear from you for a while."

His hands found hers, and his motion pulled Badger forward. Alden dropped the reins and moved his hands up so he could draw Bonnie close. Their lips met in a kiss, and she pushed away.

"Did I do something wrong?" he asked.

"No. I was afraid my father would come back."

"Maybe I should leave before he does."

She glanced over her shoulder. "Maybe so. He might be furious if he saw that I was with someone when he was gone."

Alden kissed her again but did not try to hold her except by touching her arms. When she relaxed, he said, "I'll come and see you when I can."

"Do that," she said. "Don't be a stranger."

Alden was letting Badger drink at the trough outside the way station when the front door opened. He expected to see the Professor walk out, but instead of the neatly dressed, taller-than-average man in spectacles, an unkempt, slouching man appeared. He was not wearing a hat, and his coarse hair, a dull brown, had not been cut in a while. He had dark areas beneath his eyes, an open mouth, and a stubbled face. His shirttails hung out below his jacket, and his grimy trousers ended in folds and wrinkles on his clodhopper boots. With a slow motion he raised a cigarette to his mouth and took a drag.

"Afternoon," he said.

"Good afternoon," Alden replied. "Is the Professor in?"

"Yes, he is. He's writin' letters."

"I know he had a couple of those to do."

"He seems to be workin' on a third one."

"Oh, yes. He was going to order a paper. I wonder if he needs me to take them to the post office." Alden glanced at the sun in the west. "I think there's just enough time."

"He said he'd have me do it."

Alden stole another look at the man and could find nothing familiar about him. He wondered where the man came from and how he came to speak with such ease about the Professor. "Have you been here long?" he asked.

"Came into town yesterday. Lookin' fer work." He raised his cigarette and paused before taking a drag. "Lendin' a helpin' hand to Mr. Baker right now."

The door opened, and the Professor stepped into the light. He had three envelopes in his hand. "Here you are," he said, handing them to the untidy man. "You say you know where the post office is."

"Yes, sir. Next to the barbershop."

"That's right. And here's for the postage." The Professor handed the man a silver dollar. "You should get most of that back in change. Keep two bits for yourself, and bring me the rest."

"Yes, sir."

"And here. This is Alden. Scholar on horseback. Alden, this is Orval."

Badger had finished drinking and stood with water dripping from his muzzle. Alden pulled on the reins, then turned and said, "Pleased to meet you."

The man nodded but kept his distance. "Orval Sledge. Pleased to meet you as well." To the Professor he said, "I'll be on my way. Thank you, Mr. Baker."

"Very well. I'll see you in a little while."

As the man trudged toward town, Alden said, "Is that your new helper?"

"In a small way. He looks like he tumbled off a turnip wagon, and I can't help feeling sorry for him. He said he was looking for work downtown, and a couple of fellas made fun of him."

"Some people wouldn't trust him with that much change."

"And some people have never had a fall in life. The worst he could do would be to drink up every cent in the saloon, but he doesn't seem like that type."

"Does he hope to find work on one of the ranches?"

"I don't think so. He says he's not good with horses. At least riding." The Professor gazed in the direction the man had gone. "You never know. Some men just make enough to get them to the next town or city." He came back to Alden. "And yourself? You don't seem to have gotten lured into the tents of the wicked."

Alden laughed. "I stayed away. I went on my John Alden errand." He thought for a second. "I did hear something, though. It was about Cash McGinley, or seemed to be."

"Oh?"

"He might be part of a small group that goes out and bullies the nesters on the Hermit Flats."

The Professor frowned. "What would be the purpose in that?"

"I don't know. But from the description, it seems to fit him and the horse that he rides—which horse, by the way, he still owes me for."

"Well, I haven't heard anything. If I do, I'll let you know."

"Oh, and one other thing. There's a remote possibility that someone might send me a letter in care of you. I don't expect it, but if a letter comes for me at this address, perhaps you could keep it in a safe place for me." Alden was amused at his own level of speech as he addressed the Professor.

The late afternoon sun glinted on the Professor's glasses as he tapped his hat and smiled. "I'll keep it here, as Honest Abe Lincoln was said to do."

Alden was sitting on the ground near the chuck wagon, eating noontime grub. Ben Roscoe and Jesse Burns sat nearby, also cross-legged. The aroma of boiled beans and bacon drifted on the air as the punchers clacked their spoons on their tin plates.

Ben Roscoe paused to wipe his mustache. His cream-colored hat and red bandana stood out against the background of sagebrush and grass. "Here's what I think," he said. "If a man saves half his wages for ten years, he should be able to go into business for himself. But if he works only half the year, he'll never get anywhere."

"That's good arithmetic," said Jesse. "But he's got to keep it up when he goes into business. Some fellas think they don't have to work so hard if they've got their own business. Others don't have a head for it. Like the old story about the fellas who go into the watermelon business. They get hold of a wagon, and they go out in the country and buy a load of watermelons for a dime each. They drive into town, and they set up a sign that says, 'Watermelons, ten cents.' They sell the whole wagonload, and at the end of the day, when they're sittin' on the end of the wagon countin' their money, one fella says to the other, 'Look. We worked all day, and we've got the same amount of money we started with. And we have to buy feed for the mules.' The other fella says, 'I told you we should have gotten a bigger wagon.' "

Ben said, "That's just a story."

"It is," said Jesse. "But that's how much business sense some fellas have. Some men are better off workin' for wages their whole life."

The sound of spurs caused Alden to look to his left. He saw a pair of black stovepipe boots with brown corduroy pants tucked into the tops. Farther up, he saw an ivory-handled pistol in a brown holster with a rosette stitched on it, and higher, he saw a black hat serving as a background for pale hair, a birdlike nose, and a pair of dull, brownish-green eyes the color of old pea soup. The man was directing his gaze at Ben and Jesse.

"Where's your boss?" he asked.

"He hasn't come in yet," said Jesse. He tipped back his dark, dusty hat as he looked up at the newcomer. "Something we can help you with?"

"I'm on my way through here. I've got a place on the other side of the hills, south of Silver Springs. I saw your wagon, so I thought I'd drop in."

"Glad you did," said Ben. "There's grub on the tailgate."

The visitor sniffed. "I don't have time. I need to get back to my place. I'll meet your boss some other time."

Ben said, "Shall we tell him who called?"

"My name's Cliff Worthington."

"Good of you to stop in," said Jesse. "You know where the trail is to go through the hills, don't you?"

Worthington gave him a blank stare. "Of course I do." He took in all three punchers with a glance around, and he walked away.

As the tail end of Worthington's bay horse jogged out of sight, Jesse said, "Not the friendliest sort, is he? Not to us workin' men, anyway."

Ben said, "He's new to the country, I'd guess. After he's been here for a while, he'll learn how it's good to be on friendly terms with everyone. Don't you think so, Alden? You've lived here all your life."

"It's good to get along. Maybe that was why he wanted to meet the boss." To himself, Alden wondered whether Worthington remembered him from one meeting to the next.

On the last day of roundup, the SQ boys, as Squire's hired hands were called, turned the horses into the fenced pasture and unpacked the chuck wagon. Inside the bunkhouse, Alden found two letters on his cot. His pulse quickened as he recalled his last visit with Bonnie.

The letter on top was addressed with a firm hand in ink. Alden broke the seal and unfolded the paper.

My young comrade:

I have heard a bit of news about your erstwhile friend Mr. McGinley. His body was found by a roundup crew east of the Hermit Flats and north of the breaks. Speculation has it that he was shot elsewhere and left there, though it is hard to tell. The horse he was known to ride has not been found.

I am sorry to have such news to relate, but I thought you would want to know.

Respectfully,
Cameron Baker

Alden read the letter a couple of more times and set it aside. The second letter was addressed in pencil and in uneven handwriting. Alden prepared himself for a sample of inelegant wording, but he was anxious to read it. When he opened the letter, his surprise came in the identity of the sender.

Dear Alden:

I imagine by now you have heard about Cash. I feel as if I have had the rug pulled out from under me and I do not know what to say. Not everyone has said nice things.

I know it has been a while since we talked but I trust we are still friends and I hope you will come and see me when you have time.

Claudette

Alden read Claudette's letter a couple of more times as well, then set it with the Professor's. As the news sank in, he thought of the letter he had hoped for and did not receive. It was just as well. These two were enough for one day.

CHAPTER SEVEN

Alden slowed Badger to a walk as they covered the last quarter-mile toward the bungalow. The appearance of the place had not changed since Alden's visit in the fall, with the exception that the fringes of grass were green, and instead of a horse in the corral, half a dozen reddish-brown chickens were pecking in the yard. Alden reined to a stop within a few yards of the front step, and after listening to the silence for a minute, he called out.

The door opened, and Claudette appeared, her blond hair and white apron bright in the daylight. One detail was different. She was cradling a baby in her left arm. Claudette made a small wave with her free hand and said in a raised voice, "It's good to see you. Thanks for stopping by."

Alden dismounted and walked forward so he would not have to speak in such a loud voice himself. "We just finished roundup yesterday, and that's when I got your letter. Today is a day off." He saw worry and fatigue in her facial features. "How are you holding up?"

She let out a sigh. "It hasn't been easy. This far from town, and all on my own."

"How long ago did Cash . . ."

"A little over two weeks ago."

"It must have been hard for his parents."

"They blame me, of course. I led him astray."

"And your family?"

"They haven't talked to me since I left working at the hotel. I suppose I could go back to the farm, but I'm not ready to do that yet. I'm not that far down."

He tipped his head. "What do you plan to do, then?"

Her words came as if she had rehearsed them or had said them before. "I need to make the best of a bad situation. I don't have much, but I've learned to run a house on very little."

"I'm sure you've had to."

"You know, Cash hadn't gotten the habit of working in a steady way. I think he could have, but he didn't get a chance, and that's where we are, Florence and me."

"Florence?"

"Yes." Claudette jiggled the baby, leaned her head toward it, and made a kissing sound. "She's a little girl."

Alden glanced at the baby. With its staring eyes and open drooling mouth, it looked like all other babies. He did not mind keeping what distance he had.

"Do you want to hold her?"

"No, thanks."

"That's the way Cash was. He said she was too small. He'd wait until she was a little bigger, and he wouldn't be so afraid that something would happen to her. You know, you have to be careful with a baby's head."

"I've heard that."

"Poor little baby. Never even knew her daddy, and now he's gone."

"How old is she?"

"Almost a month. Born June the eighth." Claudette turned her brown eyes full upon Alden. "Cash hardly even saw her."

Claudette did not seem to be very delicate on the subject of Cash. Alden ventured a question. "Do you have any idea of what happened to him?"

"Well, he was killed, you know. Shot twice."

"I was told some of that, but I haven't heard anything about what might have been behind it."

"No one has told me anything."

"Do you think it was related to his work?"

"I don't know what kind of work he did. He told me it wasn't good for me to know too much, so I imagine there was some danger in it. I had the idea that he was trying to catch cattle thieves, but I don't have anything specific."

"I see. In your letter you said not everybody had said kind things."

"And that's true. People have said he might have gotten shot for having sticky fingers, but I knew he didn't."

"How do you know?"

"I just know. For one thing, he never had any money. And for another, he never brought any stuff around. That's just the way people are. Someone dies under suspicious circumstances, and anyone who ever lost a pair of gloves wants to say he did it. Like that time he held the horses for that man from Shawnee—I suppose you told everyone that Cash took them."

"I never said a word about that to anyone."

"Or the horse you sold him, and he didn't have the money."

"I've mentioned that to two people, my brother, Grant, and the Professor. And it happens to be the truth."

"What does the Professor have to do with it? How does it come about that you tell him something like that?"

"It came up in conversation; that was all."

"Well, it came back to me." Claudette swivelled, as if by habit, to rock the baby.

Alden said, "I'm sorry if it did. If anyone repeated it around town, I would guess it was my brother. And even at that, like I say, it was true, and to some extent it was Grant's business. The horse belonged to our family, and now I suppose no one knows where it is."

"It hasn't been accounted for." Claudette glanced at the baby and returned to Alden. "But that's not my biggest concern."

"I can imagine."

"I have to figure out how to get along. How about you?"

Alden widened his eyes. "What do you mean?"

"What are you going to do?"

"Well, um, I guess I'll go on doing what I'm doing now. Working for wages and hoping to get somewhere."

"You're not tied down like you were before. When we talked about things last summer, you said you had to take care of your father."

Alden felt the blood rushing to his head. He thought he knew what she was leading to. "That part's true, but I don't know that I'm—"

Claudette set her lips and waited for him to finish the sentence.

He looked at his feet and up at her again. "I don't think I'm ready to take on a family."

"I see. It was all right when it was your old man you had to take care of. But I'm not good enough."

"I didn't say that. I just haven't wanted to start my own family this early in life."

She blew a breath upward. "Well, I'm not going to wait forever. There's men who'll take a woman for who she is."

"I'm sure there are. And I've got no quarrel with them."

"Fine, but don't say I didn't give you a chance."

He was surprised she was being so direct, even though she had been that way in the past. It occurred to him that her circumstances caused her to look out for herself and not miss a chance if there was one. She had to be practical. She might even have someone else in mind and wanted to know how things stood between her and Alden before she moved on.

"I wouldn't say that," he said. "If someone else comes along, there will be no hard feelings on my part."

"It's good to be clear about things," she said. "I remember one time you said you wanted to do the right thing. I think you keep your word."

"I try to." He waved the loose ends of his horse's reins. "I should be going now. If there's anything I can do to help—" He hesitated, hoping she wouldn't ask him for money.

"I think I'm all right for the time being," she said. "I've got food in the pantry, and Florence is healthy."

A feeling of guilt stole into him. Even if she had needed money, it would have been a small thing in comparison with the larger concern of Cash having been killed. Alden felt as if he had been too self-centered and was now let off the hook. "Good enough," he said. "I'll see you later."

He led Badger away, checked his cinch and set his reins, and mounted up. Turning, he waved to the young mother and her baby. Claudette waved with her free hand. Alden reined his horse around and headed toward town.

He had ridden less than a mile when he topped a rise and saw another rider coming his way. They were less than a quarter of a mile apart, and he saw no easy way for either of them to turn off the trail. Worse, Alden recognized the other man. His black hat, pale hair, and stovepipe boots were visible at a distance.

Each horse was moving at a fast walk, almost a trot, so the encounter did not last long. Alden did not look straight at the other man until the last moment, and he received but a passing glance of recognition from the greenish-brown eyes as each rider said, "Good afternoon."

Alden's heart was beating fast, and his mouth was dry. The other man was past him now. Alden sorted his thoughts and considered them in turn. Worthington was quite a ways off his range over by Silver Springs. He had been at least on speaking terms with Cash a few months back. Maybe he was just being helpful at the moment. Even if he had more of a motive than seeing to it that the bereaved woman had food in the pantry, Alden had declared that he would not harbor ill will. The best way to keep his word was not to think about other visitors very much.

Alden looked for Ben and Jesse in the Five Spot Saloon. He had no sooner hailed them than he saw his brother sitting at a table with a couple of other men. Alden excused himself from his pals and crossed the room to greet his brother.

Grant was dressed in what Alden imagined to be summer clothes. Most conspicuous was a white billed cap with a cylindrical base and a puffed-out crown that looked like a biscuit baked in a tin can. Grant also wore a bluish-grey pin-striped shirt with a small white collar and a full row of buttons down the front. He was scraping out the bowl of a curved-stem pipe. He looked up from his work and said, "Hey, if it isn't my little brother. Sit down with us, Alden."

As Alden took a seat, Grant introduced the other two men. Alden made an effort to remember the names with the features. Art Blodgett had drooping eyelids, a rough complexion, and a dusty black hat. George Oates had a brown hat, pointed ears, and a slight gap between his yellowed front teeth. As soon as the introduction was over, the two men rose from their chairs and said they had to be going. After another round of formalities, they were gone.

Grant rapped his pipe upside down on the heel of his hand. "What's new with you, Alden?"

"Not much. I worked spring roundup, and we came into town on our day off."

"I just came back to town myself. I was gone for a couple of months. Picked up some work in Cheyenne, and as usual, it ended. So I came back here to see how all of you are doing."

He held the pipe as if he was ready to fill it with tobacco. "I heard about your friend Cash McGinley. Too bad. Sounds like he might have been somewhere he shouldn't have been."

"I have no idea."

"Neither do I. Sometimes it's best not to know anything about something like that."

"It's not easy for Claudette."

"Oh, have you seen her?"

"She wrote me a letter and asked me to drop by, so I did."

"And how was that?"

"Decent, I suppose. Sometimes it seems as if she expects more out of me than I have to offer. I'm not ready for any of that—not someone else's child, and not one of my own."

"She's probably not lookin' too bad, now that she's dropped her kid."

Alden was taken aback by his brother's use of language. Alden had heard the word "dropped" only in reference to cows, when it meant giving birth. Still, he answered the implied question. "She looked about the same to me."

Grant smiled. "And you didn't find her . . . to your interest?"

"I wasn't moved, if that's what you mean. It's a bigger order than I'm interested in."

"It doesn't have to be. Sometimes it's a matter of what a fella wants and what he's willing to do to get it."

Alden shrugged. "Like I said, it's more than I care to take on."

"Hah. You might not know what to do with it anyway."

Alden sulked. When he thought of what he might or might not know to do with a girl, Claudette was not in the picture. Another girl was, and Alden was not about to tell Grant anything about her. To keep up a screen, he said, "Claudette's not a bad girl. We're still friends, and I'd help her out if I could."

"That's a good way to be. Say, can I buy you a beer?"

"No, thanks."

"Don't tell me you only drink whiskey."

Alden laughed. "All right. I can drink a glass of beer."

"One glass isn't fatal," said Grant. "A long ways from it."

The boss was laying out instructions with a pencil and a piece of paper. Ben, Jesse, and Alden were all paying attention, but the boss was directing most of his comments to Ben, who, having just observed his twenty-sixth birthday, was the oldest of the three.

"Take this main trail that goes east through the hills. It follows a dry wash for a mile or so, and then it follows a creek with running water, ponds, and some good-sized trees. That creek will curve around to the south, and the trail joins up with the Silver Springs road. Stay on that road, and you'll find yourself on kind of a narrow pass on the west side of Rawhide Mountain. The trail crosses and recrosses the creek, and you'll still see a good mix of trees—cedar, pine, box elder, cottonwood."

"I been there," said Ben. "I know what you're talkin' about."

"Good. So when you go through that narrow area, you'll come out by the south side of Rawhide Mountain. The land opens up to the south, and you can see for miles around."

"Yep."

"The road you're on meets another road." The boss drew a "T" where the roads met. "Just before you get here, on the east side of the road, a fella has a wood lot. You ought to see stacks of poles and posts he's cut along that creek and has taken off of the mountain."

"I know right where you mean."

"I've spoken for fifty cedar posts. Nothing shorter than six feet, and nothing smaller than five inches in diameter. Some of these cedar posts taper down pretty fast, from six inches to three. Don't take any of those. Tell him I said not to."

Ben rubbed his hand down over his mustache and gave a solemn nod.

"Jesse, you and Ben ride in the wagon. Alden, you ride alongside on one of your horses. If there's any trouble with the wagon, you can go for help if you-all need it. You shouldn't have any trouble, but you never know." After a pause, the boss added, "I figure a day there and a day back."

The party rolled out of the ranch before the sun had risen very high. The trail went as the boss had said, and by midday the SQ boys had come into a grassy valley between the first row of hills and the next one to the east. Rawhide Mountain rose higher than any of the other hills or buttes, as they might be called. It was also darker, with forestlike tree growth.

When the boys reached the Silver Springs road, they stopped to eat the lunch they had packed. Alden tied the dark horse to a wagon wheel and sat in the shade with his two pals.

Ben was wearing his cream-colored hat and red bandana as usual, and he seemed to have assumed his role as man in charge with some sense of importance. He took out a second handkerchief, also red, and unfolded it on his lap to catch the crumbs of bread and meat.

"Up yonder about a mile," he said, pointing north, "on a little hill, is where Mother Featherlegs is buried."

"Who's she?" asked Jesse.

"She was a roadhouse madam. Back when the Cheyenne-to-Deadwood stage was runnin', one of the routes came along this road. Another one went around the other side of Rawhide Mountain. Anyway, she had a way station here, with girls and whiskey and a no-good cutthroat named Dick the Terrapin, who came up with her from Texas. One day he took it in his head to kill her, which he did, for all the money she had on hand. About fifteen hundred dollars."

"Why did they call her 'Mother Featherlegs'?"

"As the story goes, she wore red pantalettes of a fluffy variety, so when she went riding and the wind ruffled 'em, she looked like a feather-legged chicken. She was said to have red hair, too, but I can't say that I know for sure."

"And when did this happen?" Jesse asked.

"Oh, a while back. The stage quit runnin' through here about ten years ago. Before I came to this country."

Alden spoke up. "She died in 1879, the year after I was born."

Jesse turned to him. "Is that the true story, then?"

"It's the way I've always heard it."

"Huh. And she's buried right up there. Well, this is sure a peaceful place."

"It is," said Alden, scanning the broad landscape with the breeze blowing over it. "And better grass than you see in some places over on our side."

"Just goes to show," said Ben. "And at one time, there was rotgut whiskey, painted ladies, and murderers, just a mile away."

Alden waited for an explanation of what it went to show, but Ben did not offer anything more.

The trio ate in silence for a couple of minutes until the distant thud of hoofbeats caused Alden to look to the south. Two riders were traveling at a lope.

Ben and Jesse paused in their eating as well.

Ben said, "There's still traffic on this road, anyway."

"Not to mention us," said Jesse.

As the riders approached, Alden thought he saw something familiar about the men. The one on this side wore a dusty black hat and a dark grey vest. The other wore a brown hat and a grey, buttoned-up jacket. Alden tried to remember whether he had seen them on one of the other roundup crews, and then it came to him. Blodgett and Oates. They had been sitting at

Grant's table in the Five Spot Saloon, and they had gotten up to leave when Alden arrived. Now they were riding by, each raising a gloved hand in greeting. They veered off of the Silver Springs road and followed the trail the boys had just traveled.

When the riders were a half-mile gone, Jesse said, "They don't mind raisin' a little dust while someone else is eatin'."

Ben sniffed. "I've never seen 'em before. Have you, Alden?"

"Just once, for a minute. I think my brother knows them. Now that I think of it, you two were there as well, but you had your backs to their table."

Ben raised his chin as he gazed in the distance. "You'd think they might have stopped."

"They probably didn't recognize me. And they might have thought you fellas already sold all your watermelons for the day."

Alden decided to avoid the Five Spot Saloon the next time he and the boys had a day off. He did not have a fear or even a dislike for such places, but he thought it would not be a good habit to head straight to the saloon every time he rode into town. In addition, he felt the pull of responsibility. He thought he should check in on Claudette and see how she was holding up.

Castle Butte rose in the distance as Alden rode out of town. A year ago, he had spent summer days such as this one meandering in the vicinity of the butte, watching antelope and noting the growth of grasshoppers as he kept an eye on the town herd. Now some other boy was looking after Princess and the cows, while a new generation of grasshoppers was taking the place of those that had died. At times he remembered the previous summer as a procession of carefree days, but in his more realistic memory, his days were always weighted with the worry about his father and by his boyish uncertainty about how

Claudette would treat him.

Over the last hill and with the bungalow now in sight, he focused again on the present. No horse stood at the hitching rail or in the corral. The reddish-brown chickens pecked at the ground. A magpie floated in, landed on a corral post, and flew away.

Alden rode the last quarter-mile without apprehension, at least as far as meeting up with Cliff Worthington went. He never knew what expectations or demands Claudette might put on him, but by now he had practice at resisting her.

He dismounted at his usual distance from the door and called out. After a few seconds with no response, he called again. Then came the scuff of a door opening, and a person larger than Claudette, with darker hair, appeared in the doorway. Straining his eyes, Alden recognized his brother.

Grant stepped out onto the porch in stocking feet. In a second's thought, Alden recalled how his brother, with larger feet, used to wear Alden's shoes and stretch them. When Alden complained, he would laugh.

Grant's brown hair caught the sunlight as his voice sailed out. "Well, hello, Puncher. Did you bring the mail?"

Alden said, "I didn't think to. I didn't expect to see you here."

"No harm done, I hope."

Alden assumed Claudette had told Grant about their last conversation and his pledge not to begrudge anyone. "No," he said. "I was surprised, that was all."

He noticed that his brother was wearing everyday work clothes. The entire atmosphere of the setting suggested that beyond the door, within the four walls of the little house, there was a privacy that deserved Alden's respect.

He added, "Maybe someday you'll get a telephone, and I can call ahead. They have telephones in Cheyenne, don't they?"

"They do. A fellow on a bicycle can sometimes beat the

telegraph across town, by the time they get through tapping out the message, but he's got no chance against the telephone."

"I suppose that goes for bank robbers as well as messengers."

"Most likely so, to the extent that bank robbers ride bicycles. Not bein' in the habit of doin' either, I can't tell you for sure."

Alden had thought that the caps his brother brought back from Cheyenne were the kinds of caps bicyclists wore, but he could imagine them being popular in billiard parlors and saloons as well. He had also wondered what kind of work his brother did, and he was glad to hear, at least, that it was not robbing banks. To change the subject, he said, "I saw your friends Blodgett and Oates the other day. Over on the Silver Springs road."

"What were you doing over there?"

"Riding a bicycle."

"You see more of those two than I do."

"Actually, the boss sent us over that way for a load of cedar posts."

Grant wrinkled his nose. "That means someone has to dig postholes."

Badger had put his head over Alden's shoulder, so Alden reached up and around and patted him on the cheek. With his eyes still on his brother, he said, "It's cheerful work. Every time I dig a posthole, I think of the chance that I might dig up an old chest of coins."

Grant sniffed. "You've got a better chance of diggin' up a dead Indian."

Alden thought of Mother Featherlegs and all of the people who were said to have died along the old Cheyenne-to-Deadwood stage route. He said, "Or a dead stagecoach robber."

"You're full of bank robbers and stagecoach robbers today. What have you been reading?"

"*Jack and the Beanstalk.*"

"That's a good story for growing boys. Teach 'em how to steal."

"To tell the truth, I've been reading *Great Expectations.*"

"Dickens. I don't have time for him. But I suppose it's a matter of what you get out of it. And how much time you have to kill. Are you not working very long hours now?"

"It's not like roundup, but we work plenty."

"He gives you a day off, though. Like today."

"When work is not pressing. How about yourself? Have you found work?"

"It usually finds me." Grant shifted on his feet. "I'd invite you in, but she's feedin' the baby, and the house needs to be picked up."

"That's all right. I just dropped by to see if anyone needed any help, but I can see that everything's in order."

"Just right."

"Well, I won't keep you any longer, then. I've got other errands to run."

"Good enough, Alden. Come by again when you've got time. Meanwhile, stay out of trouble."

"It helped when they quit runnin' the stage to Deadwood. I'm not tempted to go out and rob it every day."

"But there's a bank downtown, fat as a goose."

Alden smiled. "I want to stay on good terms with them."

"That's right. Even if this banker doesn't have a daughter, the next one might."

Alden stepped away from his horse and pulled the reins through his hand to straighten them. "I'm on my way, Grant. So long."

"You bet, kid. I'll see you later."

Alden did not expect to meet any other suitors on the way back to town. He figured he was the last one to know that Grant had moved in with Claudette. He told himself not to stew about the situation. Grant could take care of himself, and Claudette had someone to take care of her and the baby. Still, he could not put the new arrangement out of his mind.

By the time Alden rode into the main street, the sun was poised at the point in midafternoon that always seemed the hottest. In addition to being thirsty, Alden felt washed-out from his visit at the bungalow, and the shady interior of the Five Spot Saloon beckoned him. Seeing Ben's and Jesse's horses tied up in front, he left Badger at the hitching rail and made his way inside.

As his eyes adjusted, he found Ben and Jesse standing at the bar. When he joined them, he noted an air of relaxation about them.

"Have you boys moved since you came in here?" he asked.

"Not much," said Ben. "But we've had several interesting conversations."

Jesse said, "Not least among them, sheepherders and ticks. I never wanted to be a sheepherder, and that's one more reason." He yawned. "What time of day is it?"

"Between three and four," Alden said.

"Early yet. You've got plenty of time for a drink if you want. Where'd you go to?"

"I went to see my brother." Alden ordered a glass of beer.

"That's good," said Jesse.

"What news have you heard?"

Ben spoke. "There was a fire in Hartville. Burned two houses."

Jesse said, "Better there than here."

Alden laid a silver dollar on the bar. Beer was ten cents, and he did not expect to drink a whole dollar's worth. But he was learning how to conduct himself in these settings, and he did not want to appear stingy. "Would either of you like a drink?" he asked.

Both of his pals had more than half a glass of whiskey on the bar, and they waved away the offer as they said, "Not right now, thanks," and "Me, neither."

Alden was enjoying the effect of his first drink of beer when a voice at his side took him by surprise.

"I believe I know you."

Alden turned and drew his brows together as he tried to place the man in the dim light. Beneath the broad-brimmed brown hat, the man was suntanned and bearded.

"Bill Smith." The newcomer held out his large hand.

"From Shawnee," said Alden as he shook. "Good to see you again. You're not hunting at this time of year, are you?"

"Nah. I just took a ride down this way. I thought I might even bump into you."

"I'm glad you did. Would you like a drink?"

"Just had one. Yesterday."

"I don't think I saw you when I came in."

"You're right. And I thought I recognized that dark-eared horse at the hitchin' rail."

"I came in just ahead of you, then. This is my first drink."

Bill shrugged as if to say that no one needed to account to him. Then, with as casual an air as if he was looking for a place to buy fishing line, he said, "I heard your pal Cash McGinley got rubbed out."

"That's what I heard, too. I was out working roundup at the time." Alden expected Bill Smith to make a comment about Cash's sticky-fingered tendencies or to ask a question about how he died, but the man was as unceremonious as ever.

"What about that girl he had livin' with him?"

Alden realized Bill knew that much, that they weren't married. Aloud, he said, "She's taken up with someone else."

"Is he any better than the first one?"

"I'd like to think so. He's my brother." Alden took a drink from his glass. "Are you sure you wouldn't like a drink?"

"Thanks all the same. I'm plannin' to go back, and a hot day like this can bake your brains if you've had too much to drink."

"Well, it's been good to see you. Have a safe trip."

"I hope to. Maybe I'll see you in the fall. Thanks for telling me what you know."

"You're welcome." Alden wanted to say that it seemed like the right thing to do, but he thought it wouldn't make that much of a difference to Bill Smith, so he said, "Any time."

CHAPTER EIGHT

A cold wind blew from the northwest, and daylight struggled through a grey sky. A hawk skimmed low over the dull, dry grass and lifted away with the crosscurrent of air. Alden hunched his shoulder against the cold as he rode toward the town of Morse. The best part of autumn had passed in a blink, it seemed, with the hurried work and shortening days of fall roundup. With the wind on his cheek and his bedroll tied to his saddle, he felt as if he was riding back into the austere world of last winter, with the exception that he had wages in his pocket.

Not being broke made a difference. A bit of money gave him a feeling of security, but he knew he needed to put it in a safe place, not let it trickle away. He hoped he did not have to live hand-to-mouth again, but he told himself he could not consider himself above menial work. He had a purpose he was working toward, even though time seemed to roll away from him like the prairie beneath the hooves of a galloping horse.

With the Squire Ranch at his back and with a sense of having ridden away from it, he directed Badger to the way station. The Professor always knew something. Maybe he would know of a situation, and if he didn't, Alden could ask him to keep an ear open.

The water trough was half-full, with a tumbleweed lodged in one end. After dismounting, Alden saw that the stem was stuck in a floe of ice. The sight served as a reminder of what time of year it was, when a person did not fill the trough all the way so that he could pour fresh water on top if the tank froze solid. With his gloved hand, Alden lifted the prickly tumbleweed and its small sheet of ice and tossed the combination away. As he stepped aside to let Badger drink, a movement at the station door caught his eye.

Orval Sledge stepped out of the building, wearing a coarse wool overcoat but no hat. The wind ruffled his dull brown hair, and he leaned his head forward. His posture, along with the dark areas beneath his eyes, a ten-day stubble on his face, and an open mouth, gave him a primitive appearance that Alden found interesting to observe.

Orval put his hands in his coat pockets and hunched against the wind. "Not yer best kind of weather," he said.

"It's that time of year."

"Winter's right around the corner."

"We've got November first. That's when the wind blows all day and on through the night."

"Yep." Orval shifted a toothpick in his mouth without taking his hands from his pockets.

Alden had more to say about the weather, but he decided to let it pass. He said, "I thought I'd drop in on the Professor on my way into town."

"He ain't here."

"Oh, I see. So you're—"

"Lendin' a helpin' hand."

"That's good. Well, it looks as if my horse has had his drink, so I guess we'll be moving along. I'll drop in on the Professor later on, maybe tomorrow."

"If he's here, you'll find him."

"Thanks." Alden led Badger away, snugged the cinch, and mounted up. Glancing over his shoulder, he saw Orval Sledge, chin jutted forward, studying the water trough. The man had a knack for stating the obvious and the obscure at the same time, and Alden wondered what he saw in the murky water.

The buildings downtown did not block out much of the wind but rather seemed to create channels of rushing air. Alden had to tip his head to keep his hat on as he led Badger to the hitching rail in front of the bank. Once he stepped up onto the sidewalk and into the lee of the building, the wind diminished. Pulling himself together, Alden walked into the bank.

The teller with wire-rimmed glasses, slicked-back hair, a pointed nose, and a close-trimmed mustache gave him a look of scrutiny as if a person behind the window in a bank needed to be wary of someone who had just blown in off the range.

Alden put his hands on the counter and said, "I'd like to deposit some money."

The teller pursed his lips and gave Alden a second looking-over. "Do you have an account with us?"

"No, I don't, but I've been in here before. My name's Alden Clare."

"Very well. You'll have to open an account." The teller reached under the counter and brought out a printed sheet of paper. After lifting a pen from the inkwell, he wrote Alden's name on the first line. Looking up, he said, "Address?"

"I don't have one right now. I just finished a season of work, and I've come into town. You could put it as General Delivery."

The teller breathed out what seemed like a small huff of impatience. "Date of birth?"

"August seventeenth, eighteen-seventy-eight."

The teller wrote the information in the appropriate blank. "Next of kin?"

"My brother, Grant Clare." Alden pondered the possibility of coming to an early death. He stopped at the idea of his money going toward city clothes for his brother or candy for Cash McGinley's daughter.

"And how much would you like to deposit today?"

"A hundred-and-fifty dollars."

The teller's eyebrows flickered. Alden wondered if the man had expected him to deposit five dollars.

"Do you have it in cash?"

"Right here."

When the transaction was finished, Alden looked past the teller and said, "It looks as if Mr. Dorrance is in."

"He is."

"I wouldn't mind imposing on a minute of his time, if I could."

The teller raised his eyebrows. "What would it be a question about? Maybe I can answer it."

"No question. Just a word of greeting."

"I'll convey it."

Alden took in a breath to steady himself. "I'd like to say it in person, if I could."

The teller looked at Alden as if he was reading the amount of deposit on his young face. "I'll see."

A moment later, Newton Dorrance came striding out of his office with his bald head shining and his coattails flowing. He stood at the counter where the half-door was latched. "Good day, good day," he said. "Welcome to the fold."

Alden moved sideways to stand opposite the banker. "Thank you, sir. It's not much to begin with, but I'm saving toward a good purpose."

The smiling man put out his hand, and as the two of them shook, he said, "You've got a lot of heart, boy." His bushy white mustache relaxed, and his ruddy cheeks glowed.

"Thank you."

Within seconds, both the banker and the teller returned to their work, and Alden was left to himself. Rather than try to exchange any further courtesy with the teller, he turned away and walked outside.

He stood on the sidewalk for a minute, gathering his thoughts before venturing again into the wind. He had a sense of satisfaction, even pride, in having put away such a sum of money toward his good purpose. At the same time, he felt something nagging. He thought it was natural for the teller and the banker to condescend to him, but as he considered the exchange he had just gone through, he thought he had been too willing to ask for the banker's approval. A word came to him from his reading: *obsequious.* He had put himself below those men.

He stepped down into the street and patted his horse on the neck. At least he was himself again. His embarrassment should be a small matter, and he imagined he was the only one who thought any more about the meeting.

Still, he felt edgy, uneasy. He did not want to talk to anyone else at the moment, and he did not have in mind a place where he wanted to go right away. He was hungry, as he so often was, but he needed to put off buying a meal. He had decided he would pay for one cooked meal per day and eat cold food the rest of the time. He did not want to use up his one indulgence too early in the day.

He decided to wear off some of his uneasiness by walking up and down the street. Sometimes exercise put off his hunger for a while. He laughed to himself. Sometimes it just made him hungrier.

He untied the reins and led Badger into the street. The wind was blowing in irregular gusts, whipping up small clouds of dirt and debris. He tipped his head one way and another into the wind. On one such movement, he caught sight of the Professor standing inside Julia Redwine's dry goods store. The two of them stood in a pose of amiable conversation. For a moment it seemed to Alden as if that was the privilege of being an adult— being comfortable and at ease, with no apparent problems. Then he recalled how Julia, a widow, had one obligation after another to tend to. Even the Professor, who seemed so carefree, had made his remarks about having gone through disappointment and having had a fall in life.

Alden looked back at his horse. All he had to care for was the two of them, and he had a bit of money in his pocket as well as a small, tidy amount in the bank. He reminded himself that he did not need to be in a hurry for the privileges of adulthood.

After a couple of trips up and down the center of town, he felt as if he had earned his dinner. He tied Badger at the rail in front of the café and went in.

He took a seat at a small side table, not far from the center table where Grant had been putting away a plate of ham and eggs several months earlier. The table, empty now, gave Alden a combined sense of his brother's presence and absence.

Alden ordered a bowl of beef stew, which came with a small plate of biscuits. Although he felt a sharp hunger, he took his time, not wolfing his food as he had seen so many working men do.

He finished his bowl and ordered a second one. He was making his way through it when the front door opened and the Professor walked in. His head tipped up in recognition, and he walked toward Alden's table.

The Professor was dressed in dark brown, as he often was, with a short-brimmed hat, a wool vest and coat, and wool pants. His shirt was clean and white, and his thin gold watch chain was shining. He stopped in front of Alden and turned his hand palm up.

"Mind if I join you?" he asked.

"Please do."

As he took a seat, he said, "I didn't know you were in town until I saw you walking in the street."

"We're done for the season. Got the steers shipped and everything put away. I came into town a little earlier. I stopped in to see you, but your helper said you weren't in. So I went about my errands."

"I let him mind the store for an hour even when there's no need."

"He seems to take it seriously."

"No harm to him as near as I can see. He doesn't have an ounce of guile."

Alden considered the comment and nodded in agreement as he poised his spoon. "Is there any news?"

The Professor gave a mild shrug. "Not in the way of public doin's. No weddings, no deaths, no big upheavals that I can think of. Things are pretty quiet now, with the cattle season ended, like you said."

"Just as well."

"One little thing did come up, which is why I came in here to interrupt your meal."

Alden paused with his spoon at the edge of the bowl. "Go ahead."

"Nothing catastrophic. Rather, it might be an opportunity for you."

"Oh?"

"There's a man who has a small ranch north of here, and he needs someone to look after his place for the winter. He needs to go home and tend to other interests, and I don't think he wants to go through a hard winter here."

"Where's he from?"

"Virginia. But you wouldn't know it to talk to him. He doesn't have that smooth accent they have."

"What's his name?" Silver Springs was east, not north, but Alden still had an apprehension.

"Miller. He says he'll pay ten dollars a month."

"That's not much."

"There's not much work. Look after a couple of horses, keep

saddle tramps and squatters from moving in. You'd have a place to stay, and time to do other things."

"I don't know what else I could do if I was stuck there. Maybe a little bit of hunting. I don't care for trapping. And I'd like to make more money."

The Professor shrugged. "You could do like some fellows do. Go out and brand mavericks on the *q.t.* Or you could write wholesome stories for young boys."

"Like Horatio Alger."

"Something like that. A bootblack works his way up in the world and comes to own an ink factory." The Professor's grey eyes had a merry expression behind the lenses of his spectacles.

"How soon does it start?"

"Right away. Miller left a couple of days ago, and he has a neighbor dropping in until we can do better. I told him I thought I could find someone. If you can't do it, I might be able to put Orval at it, but I don't know how he would get back and forth by himself, much less do any riding on the place if it was necessary."

"I'd like to find something that pays better, but I suppose I could do it. Ten dollars a month is more than I made last winter."

"Think it over for a day or two," said the Professor. "Miller didn't plan for this very well ahead of time. I think he might not have expected to leave for the winter, and then when he got a sample of the weather, he changed his mind."

Alden still had his spoon poised. "And we're not into November yet."

"It's not far away. Go ahead and eat. Don't let your stew get cold."

Weak sunlight straggled through a gossamer cloud cover, and a light breeze from the northwest chilled the air. Alden was sure the temperature was below freezing, but no frost had formed on the dry grass. Badger's hooves made a soft crunching sound to combine with the light, dull thuds of footfall. With leather gloves and a blanket-lined canvas coat, Alden felt at ease in the weather. Moreover, he felt a kinship with the spareness of the rangeland, where the plant life did not grow very high and wildlife was making itself scarce. He had seen one antelope, a speck of tan and white, in the direction of Castle Butte, but now even the butte itself was closed off from view by the gradual rise and fall of the landscape.

Ahead of him, the Hermit Flats did not promise a great change, with the exception that he hoped he would be able to see Bonnie. As he counted back, he realized he had not seen her for five months. The work season had passed as if in an instant, in spite of long days of drudgery, and on the two occasions when he had had a day off, he had tended to what he thought was his responsibility with Claudette. With some chagrin, he realized how little time he had been allowed for himself and how little he had gotten out of it.

On the other hand, his feelings for Bonnie had not changed. Their last meeting seemed like yesterday, and he thought it natural that she would feel the same as before. Still, he told himself not to take anything for granted. For all he knew, a punkin roller might have made his pitch, sidling up to Jack Wilcox with a bottle of whiskey and gaining the privilege of dropping by.

Alden rode on, playing out one scenario and then another, until the Wilcox homestead came into sight. It did not look much different from before. What little green grass had been showing in late spring had gone dead, and nothing new had appeared in the form of buildings.

Seeing no one outside, Alden was not sure how to approach the place. Calling out might save him the discomfort of meeting

Jack Wilcox face-to-face at the door and being turned away, but it might also give Jack the opportunity to look out, tell his daughter to stay put, and send the visitor away. On the other hand, if Alden knocked, Bonnie might answer the door. It was a fifty-fifty chance, but Alden did not like what seemed like the bigger half. He decided to call out. If he was going to be turned away by Jack Wilcox, he would rather it be from a distance.

He brought Badger to a stop, rose in his stirrups, and put the flat of his hand next to his mouth. "Yoo-hoo! Anyone home?"

He settled into his seat and watched the door. After a moment, he called again and continued watching the door.

Movement on the left caught his eye. Neither Bonnie nor Jack appeared, but rather Sooters, dressed in an oversized pullover sweater and a pair of loose trousers. His hair was not long, but it was untrimmed and uncombed, and his face had the filmy quality of not having been washed in a while. He turned in the direction he had come from, and with his arms cocked at his sides, he hollered.

"Bonnie! It's that guy!"

As Alden waited, Sooters stayed where he was and stared. Alden made a routine smile, and getting no response, sat with his hands on the saddle horn. A minute passed, then another.

Movement flickered, and Bonnie appeared around the corner, behind Sooters. She wore a grey wool coat with the cuffs turned up, denim trousers, and brogan shoes. She walked past the boy into the open and raised her hand to shade out the pale sunlight.

"Hello," she said. "This is a surprise."

"Good morning." Alden swung down from the saddle and took a couple of steps toward her.

She lowered her hand, as she no longer had to look up into the sun. Her hair was tied back, and she had an open, pleasant expression on her face. "It's been a while." She glanced at Sooters and back at Alden. "My father and Paul Sherwood are off on some kind of business for the day, so Sooters is looking after me. We were bringing in firewood." She turned. "Sooters, why don't you take the wheelbarrow back to the woodpile, and I'll be with you in a couple of minutes."

Sooters put on a sullen look. "It's your job. I'm just helping."

"Oh, come on. I'll wheel it back when it's full."

"They told me to keep an eye out."

"You can still do that. Come on. Someday you'll want me to do something for you."

"I don't know what."

"Not now, you don't. But you know I'm right. And it'll only be for a few minutes."

Sooters gave a long, slow stare at Alden and his horse, then returned to Bonnie. Alden could tell he was giving up.

"All right," said Sooters. "But if anything happens—"

"Nothing will. I'll be there before you have the wheelbarrow loaded."

Sooters turned and walked away with a heavy-footed gait.

Bonnie smiled at Alden. "I'm sorry I didn't write, but I didn't find a way."

Alden moved a couple of steps forward with Badger at his elbow. "I'm sorry I didn't come out to see you, but I've had only a couple of days off. I got stuck doing other things, and then I didn't have enough time. It's a long ride. It takes the whole middle part of the day."

"I know." She smiled again. "But you're here, so that's what counts."

He looked past her and spoke in a low voice. "Do you think he went away, or is he around the corner listening?"

She drew her brows together. "That's the sound of the wheelbarrow. We should hear him dropping in the firewood in a minute."

"You seem to get along all right with him."

"We're almost like brother and sister. I don't mind it. He's like the little brother I never had."

Alden hesitated, not wanting to seem too curious. "Then you've never had brothers or sisters at all?"

She shook her head. "My father was gone for periods of time when I was little, and then my mother died. I think she wore herself down with fret and worry, and with having to provide for me."

"I'm sorry to hear that."

She gave a light shrug. "I've learned that you have to take what life hands you."

"So have I. Up to a point, anyway."

Her eyes held still. "I'm not sure what you mean."

"Well, I don't mean to say that I've had it as hard as you have, or that you shouldn't have had to take what you were given. What I mean is that I'm at a point where I make my own choices, and I hope I can determine, to some extent, the direction I go in."

Her face relaxed. "You sound like you think about things and don't just barge into them."

"I try."

"You have an intelligent way of talking. I have a hunch that you read things you can learn from."

"I try to do that, too. When I read a book, I learn about ideas and . . . I guess, higher things. Not just spuds and turnips. Those things are important, too, but they're not everything. It seems as if too much of our life is taken up by not having enough money and by trying to do something about it."

Her dark eyes opened wide. "That's exactly the truth. And I wonder if that's the way things are always going to be."

"That's why I hope a person can determine some of his own life. Decide what's important, and try not to make it all about money and what money can buy."

"It sounds easy when you talk about it."

"Yes, it does. But a person ought to be able to rise above the things that drag so many people down." He felt lifted by his own words. "Just in my own case and those around me, I've seen it, and I don't want it to happen to me."

A shadow seemed to pass over her face. "You mention those around you. Do you have a family?"

"My father died about a year ago. My mother died quite a bit earlier, when my brother and I were small."

"Your brother."

"Yes. I have just one. His name is Grant. I haven't seen him in a while, either, what with my work and all."

Bonnie drew her mouth together in a thoughtful expression. "I believe I've heard something about him."

"Oh, what's that?"

"I think he took the place of the boy who was found dead. Cash McGinley."

Alden felt a wave of uneasiness. He did not know how to talk about people who lived together without being married, especially to a girl. He said, "I don't know exactly how it happened. I went away to work, and when I came back, they were together."

"Who? Him and Cash?"

"No. Grant and Claudette."

"I don't know anything about her."

Alden frowned. "Then I don't know what you mean about his taking Cash's place."

"With the troublemakers," she said.

Alden let the awareness sink in. "Ohhh," he said, in a long syllable. He felt as if he had come back to earth after his philosophizing. Moreover, he felt as if he had to answer for his brother. "I didn't know what he was doing for work or whatever it is."

"He rides with two of the rough ones that the other boy rode with."

"And how did you know he was my brother?"

"I heard his name mentioned. I just overheard it. No one said it for my benefit."

Alden thought for a couple of seconds. "And the other two?"

"I don't think I've heard their names."

"Does one of them have drooping eyes, and the other has pointed ears?"

"One has eyes like you say. He comes closer than the others. Close enough that you can smell him. But he thinks he's a charmer. Even while he's out here bullying people, he'll show up when I'm doing chores by myself, and he tells me I ought to think about giving up on slopping the hogs. And we don't even have hogs. But his idea is clear. I don't say a word to him."

"So much the better. Is that why your father and Paul Sherwood leave Sooters here with you?"

"That, and things in general."

"Like me. Has your father said anything about Grant being my brother?"

"Not to me."

Alden let out a sigh. "I feel as if I have to eat my own words about having a say in what happens to a person." He shrugged as he felt his confidence coming back. "It's still a good idea. We just have to grow into that stage where we have more of a hand in things." He met her eyes. "I have a resistance to trying to grow up too fast—something else I've seen in others."

"I know what you mean," she said. "Some people get impatient, like Mr. Sherwood talked about that day." She gave a slight frown and turned her head. "I don't hear Sooters loading any more firewood."

Alden realized he had been hearing the clunking sounds and now he didn't. "Does that mean you have to go?"

"Probably so. And I don't know when my father's coming back, anyway."

All of the intervening time vanished, and this moment was a continuation of an earlier one. His hands met hers, then released as he put his arms around her. Their kiss was longer this time, and their separation less abrupt.

"I'll be thinking of you," he said.

"So will I."

She turned, and he followed her gaze. Sooters stood at the corner of the house, staring.

"Are you ready?" Bonnie asked.

Sooters did not speak.

"Don't let your eyes bug out," she said. "Go ahead. I'm right behind you."

"You said that last time."

"Well, I am now." She smiled to Alden and said, "Goodbye."

"Goodbye," he answered.

"Don't stay away so long."

"I won't."

As Bonnie followed Sooters to their work, Alden led Badger away. He pulled the cinch and mounted up. Badger stepped out, and Alden was left to his thoughts once again. It was a long ride out and back for a few minutes of company, but he was happy for the minutes he had.

Alden reached the way station as the setting sun was leaving a yellow-orange sky in its wake. The shortest days of the year were still more than six weeks away, but even now he noticed the days becoming shorter on each end, and a chill set in as soon as the sun went down. This year's grasshoppers were dead, and the ants had gone underground. Alden told himself that if he had any sense, he had better be seeking a shelter as well.

A lamp was shining inside the station, so Alden tied his horse and went in. The Professor turned in his chair and set aside a book with a faded brown cloth binding.

"The curfew tolls the knell of parting day," he said. " 'Tis well that you should drop in, and not become a borrower of the night."

"Are you practicing your recitations?"

"Those are from two separate pieces, as you may know. The sunset was melancholy enough that I was touched by the poetic spirit." The Professor blinked from behind his glasses. "As for practicing, I don't get to do much of it with Orval." He tapped his fist against his chest. "And sometimes it has to speak out."

"I understand."

"So, is there anything in particular that brings you in at this pensive hour?"

Alden smiled. "Nothing very poetic. But if the offer from yesterday is still good, I'd like to take the situation of looking after the man's ranch."

"Miller? Glad to hear it. A small benefit on both sides. As for the poetic spirit, you might find the solitude very amenable. With a volume of graveyard poetry and a volume of Shakespeare, you could weather out a long storm."

"As far as that goes, it has occurred to me that I could do some reading."

"Have you anything in mind? *Bleak House,* perhaps?"

Alden recalled seeing the book, and he thought it was the thickest novel he had ever seen. "I think I'm caught up on Dickens, though I like him very much."

"Well, if you think of a title, let me know. I might have it. Or you could look over what I have, and you could decide if there's anything you'd like to try."

"I'll keep that in mind. Would it be good enough if I started taking care of the Miller place tomorrow?"

"That should be fine. Drop by here, and I'll get out the

instructions and the map."

"Is it that hard to find?"

"I didn't know who I was going to send. Or I should say *whom*."

CHAPTER NINE

Alden sat in the doorway of the Miller shack and gazed out at the empty grassland. Having taken a look at the ranch, as it was called, he mulled over what his job would entail. The property consisted of half a section, three-hundred-and-twenty acres, with a three-wire fence to keep all the neighboring cattle out and two horses in. Miller had no cattle. For buildings he had a small house, a low stable, and an outhouse.

The dwelling measured about twenty feet square and had a pyramid roof with uneven wooden shingles. Inside, it had a front room, a bedroom, a kitchen, and a small pantry. Miller had rolled up his mattress and his bedding into two bundles and had hung them from the bare rafters with telegraph wire. A sheet-iron stove provided the only heat. A small stack of firewood, with no pieces more than three inches thick, rested along one wall. Alden had not seen any other firewood on the place.

The stable, about eight feet by sixteen, was made of unpainted rough lumber. A sagging door hung on leather hinges. On the east side, an overhang offered shelter for the horses. Inside the shed, a fifty-gallon barrel was three-quarters full of oats. A warped sheet of tin, two feet square and held down by a rock the size of a loaf of bread, served as a lid to keep out rats.

The outhouse had neither lime nor newspapers. An empty wasp nest hung in one corner.

By Alden's calculation, he had enough firewood for three

days and enough oats for three weeks. He imagined he was responsible for finding more firewood. He would ask the Professor about the grain. He would also have to figure a way for transporting those supplies.

For a short while, he resented Miller. The man had done one thing that was an adequate provision against the winter, and that was to hang the mattress and bedding with telegraph wire, which everyone did in every line shack, cabin, or homestead shanty that would lie vacant in the winter. Other than that precaution, the man had gone off like a gentleman or absentee landowner and had left the responsibilities to someone else.

Alden had an urge to do the same, except that he knew the horses needed to have water. They could get by without grain, biting off the grass lower than a cow could, but unless they ran free, someone had to put water in the trough, break ice, and even chop out blocks when the whole thing froze solid. At the end of Alden's ruminations, it was the horses' need for water that softened him. He would stay for them, and if things became impossible, he could take them into town or set them free to fend for themselves.

Having a plan, if only a vague one, cheered him up. He did not know how far the ten dollars a month would stretch, or where he was going to find firewood, but he was not helpless. He could do his work.

The water trough had a quarter-inch sheet of ice in the morning, and the horses had made a hole for drinking. With the flat end of the ax head, Alden broke the ice into several pieces. The water below was clear, though the slimy green walls of the wooden trough gave it a gloomy cast.

Alden put the ax in the shed. He figured the horses were good for water for the rest of the day, so he was free to tend to his own affairs. Since the conversation with Bonnie the day before, a new sense of obligation had visited him from time to time. It came with a sense of dread, but he knew he should visit his brother.

With the wire gate shut behind him, Alden left the Miller place at midmorning. He had a clear sense of direction. Castle Butte lay to the southwest, and town lay to the southeast. If he rode in a straight line toward Grant and Claudette's place, he would miss town by about a mile on the west side. He estimated the total distance at less than ten miles, so he felt no need to push Badger beyond a fast walk.

The bungalow came into view at a different angle than he was used to, but he rode around and approached it from his usual direction. Smoke was threading up out of the stovepipe, and chickens were pecking in the yard. At the approach of a horse and rider, a solid brown horse in the corral raised his head over the top rail and let out a neigh.

As Alden drew rein, the front door opened. Grant stepped outside, putting on a winter cap like the one he had worn at home. He puffed out his chest and called, "Hey, little brother. You came for a visit."

Alden dismounted and stood with the reins behind him. "That's right. We finished the season at the Squire, and I took on a little obligation for the winter."

"A squaw?"

"I'm looking after a place for a fellow who's gone. Name of Miller. North of town and a little ways to the west."

"Huh. What's it pay?"

Alden thought the question was a bit blunt, but he gave a direct answer. "Ten dollars a month."

"Starvation wages."

"It's not much work, and it gives me a place to stay."

"There's easier ways to get by. At least last winter you were a stone's throw from the middle of town."

"I just thought I would let you know where I was."

"Sure." After a pause, Grant said, "Why don't you tie up and come in? We just ate, but Claudette could fix you something if you wanted."

"I'm not hungry, thanks." Alden's stomach seemed to groan in awareness. He wondered how long he would stay and whether the offer would come around again.

Inside, the house smelled of tobacco smoke and dirty laundry, with a trace of what Alden thought was baby laundry. Claudette stood with her back to Alden, holding Florence on her left hip as she stacked dishes with her free hand. She looked over her shoulder and smiled.

"How," she said.

Alden wondered at her easy familiarity, as if they saw each other every few days and she hadn't taken up with his brother. "Afternoon," he said.

Grant pulled a chair away from the table, making a scraping sound. As he sat down, he said, "It's not twelve yet. Lacking a few minutes. Have a seat."

As Alden took a chair, he saw a whiskey bottle and a glass in front of his brother.

"Care for a drink?"

"No, thanks. Isn't it a bit early?"

"It's my first one. And there's nothin' else to do."

"I didn't know if you had a job."

"I pick up work here and there." Grant pulled open a sack of Bull Durham and began to make a cigarette. Alden sensed an air of authority as his brother troughed the paper and shook out the grains of tobacco. Grant pulled the string with his teeth and said, "Our old place is still empty."

Alden noted the change in topic. "I haven't gone by there."

"Nothin's changed. They could have a band of gypsies stayin'

145

there, and no one would know." Grant kept his eye on his work as he rolled the cigarette.

"That's one thing Miller was worried about. Squatters."

"Pah. For what?"

"It's not the poorest land around. Ours, that is, or even his, for that matter. There's worse, and people seem to want to fight over it."

Grant licked the seam and tapped it. He did not look up, but his eyebrows were raised.

Alden went on. "Like the Hermit Flats. I know a girl out there, and she tells me her folks and the neighbors are bothered by men who try to run them off."

Grant flipped the cigarette into his mouth and lit it with a sweep of his hand. He shook out the match, blew a stream of smoke, and said, "So what?"

"I don't know what the purpose is. And it seems to be related to the way Cash came to an end." Alden stole a glance at Claudette, but she did not show any reaction.

Grant said, "He got killed because he was stupid, that's what."

Alden dared to push a little further. "In what way?"

Grant answered in slow, separate syllables. "He went too far."

"Well, I wish people wouldn't do things like that."

"What? Go too far?"

"Not just that, but hectoring those people to begin with."

"Are you sweet on that girl?"

Alden was set back for a second. "I wish people wouldn't give them trouble."

"It's her old man that's the trouble." Grant took another drag. "I don't suppose you're friends with him."

"Not much. But he knows who's who."

"Oh, and so it goes rough on you. I didn't know you even knew the girl. But it doesn't change things." Grant took a drink from his glass of whiskey and stretched his upper lip over his teeth.

"Maybe I'll speak more clearly," said Alden. "As far as her old man goes, I don't care much about him. But I don't like to see anyone torment her. And besides, I don't want anything to happen to you."

Grant snorted. "I'm not stupid like some people."

"Why do you even do it?"

"It's not the only thing I do. It's part of my job."

"Look," said Alden. "You can find other work. We can go in together, and we can try to get our own place back. I've got a little money set aside already."

"That place was never worth much anyway, and you know it. Just a place to work for nothin'." Grant took another drag. "It's not easy to make a living when the biggest thing around is a one-horse cowtown. I've got a wife and a kid to look after, and I'm not gonna do something just because someone wants me to. So if that's why you came here, you can forget it."

"I didn't know you were married."

"Would it make a difference if I was?" Grant picked up his glass and swirled the whiskey.

"Then you're not."

"What difference does it make?"

"None to me, I guess."

"Jesus," said Grant. "You're as bad as the old man. You get a hold of something, and you won't leave it alone." He took a drink. "What else is on your mind today?"

Alden wished he could ask his brother outright who his boss was, but he could not see a way to do it. "Nothing more I can think of," he said.

"Well, there's no need to stay mad. Would you like something to eat?"

"No, thanks. I'm still not hungry." This time, Alden was telling the truth.

Badger looked on as Alden brushed the first of the two Miller horses, a swaybacked sorrel. Its partner, also a sorrel but with a lighter build and a straighter back, stood dozing where it was tied at the same rail. After his initial dismay at his new situation, Alden decided he might make use of one or both of the horses to haul grain and firewood as the need came up.

He set aside the brush and took up the steel comb. As he reached for the horse's mane, the animal stamped. Alden stepped back, keeping his toes clear, and looked the horse over. He saw no deer flies or horse flies, which were often the cause of an animal stamping when it was tied up. Even this late in the year, a few insects lingered, especially flies and wasps. Alden pulled the slip knot so that the horse was no longer tied snug. Until he knew the horses better, he did not want to risk pulling the hitching rail loose or spooking the other horse. Alden went back to combing the mane, and the horse kept still.

Alden kept an eye on the animal's front feet. The hooves were as broad as a pair of small cast-iron skillets, and each pastern had white hair growing down over the coronet band. This was a heavy-built horse but not bad-looking, with its reddish coat, two white socks, and a clear white blaze. A glance at the other sorrel showed him that it had four white socks and a white underside to its chin. Those were good details to remember. They would help him tell the horses apart in the dark.

When the time came to put on the saddle, the heavyset animal did not flinch. Alden tightened the cinch and led the horse out on a walk. He did not see a need to step into the saddle. He guessed that the horse had been ridden in the past month or so, but he was a long ways from town to find out that a devious beast was waiting for him to step aboard. A good way to try out a horse, or to get him accustomed to a saddle and weight, was to tie a sack of grain onto the saddle. Because that was one use he expected to put the horse to anyway, he decided he could wait until he had grain to haul.

The sorrel hung his head and let out a sigh.

Oh, hell, thought Alden. *If this horse is anything but a plug, I'll be surprised.*

He tried the bridle, and the horse took the bit right into its mouth. Alden settled the headstall around the ears, set his reins, and snugged the near one. When the sorrel stepped back on its left front foot and turned its head inward, Alden had his hands on the saddle horn and his toe in the stirrup. He swung his right leg up and over and settled into the seat. Unlike horses that always had a tension, like Buttermilk, this one was as steady and calm as Badger. Alden walked him out in a series of loops and figure-eights, and when he took him back to the rail and dismounted, the horse sighed again.

Docile, thought Alden. If he ever needed a horse for a girl to ride, this one would do fine.

Alden walked out of the general store with ten pounds of potatoes in a burlap sack and a three-pound slab of bacon wrapped in brown paper. He recalled the dwindling stack of firewood in the kitchen, enough to cook one more meal. With so few trees in this part of the country to begin with, and none within view of the Miller homestead, he would have to find a place that had not been picked clean. His mind went back to the trip he had taken with Ben and Jesse to the south end of Rawhide Mountain. There he had seen stacks of fence posts and corral poles, with mounds of firewood lying around like so much refuse. He shook his head as he thought of the abundance. He had read stories of men suffering from thirst and dreaming of rivers and lakes and waterfalls. Hungry men envisioned cakes and pies and chunks of roasted meat, baskets of bread and platters of golden fried chicken. Alden smiled. Right now, he would be satisfied with another three days' supply of firewood, enough to cook a pot of beans as well as to fry spuds and boil coffee.

He stopped at the sight of a horse he thought he recognized. A brown horse like the one in Grant's corral stood tied to the hitching rail in front of the Five Spot Saloon. Alden glanced at the sky, reminding himself of the hour—a little after one o'clock. He tied his provisions onto the back of the saddle and made his way across the street to the saloon.

Inside, he blinked a couple of times as his eyes adjusted. He recognized his brother by the cap he wore. Grant was sitting at a table by himself with a bottle and a glass in front of him. Smoke curled up from a cigarette tucked into the fingers of his hand that rested on the glass. His eyes were relaxed in a gaze off in the middle distance through the lamplight and cigarette smoke. He perked up as Alden moved into his line of vision, and he gave an easy smile that Alden associated with the contents of the glass. His voice had some of the edges knocked off as well.

"Hey, Puncher. What's in the wind?"

"I saw your horse, so I thought I'd drop in. I didn't expect to see you here."

Grant's expression cleared up, and his voice took on some of its more usual sharpness. "I'm not one to sit up against the sunny side of a building and shell peanuts."

"Are you waiting for a card game?"

"Hah. Could be. How about yourself?"

"I came into town to buy a little grub. I need to look for firewood after I get back. Miller didn't leave much of a supply."

Grant curled one nostril. "Boys in Cheyenne would go out at night and pilfer coal from the train yard."

"That's up to them."

"It keeps a fire going."

"Well, there's no train yard around here, anyway."

"But there's coal. They bring it down from Shawnee. Your friend could tell you about it." Grant put his cigarette to his mouth, and the tip glowed.

Alden's brows tightened. "What do you know about him?"

Grant laughed. "Just that Cash tried to get away with his horses. Another one of his stupid moves. Why don't you sit down?"

"I guess I could." Alden took a chair at a right angle from his brother.

"What else is new?"

"Nothing since I saw you two days ago. And yourself?" Alden raised his hat and scratched the back of his head.

"The same." Grant rotated his glass, and the smoke rose from his cigarette.

Alden was trying to think of a topic of conversation when two men walked into the saloon. The door closed and cut off the daylight, but not before Alden recognized Blodgett and Oates. Their spurs jingled and their bootheels clomped as they walked toward the table.

Grant looked up at them with a calm expression and said, "Afternoon, boys. Have a seat."

Alden thought, *That's what he was waiting for.*

As the two men sat down, Grant said, "You remember my brother, Alden."

"Seen him," said Blodgett, rubbing his hand across his rough chin. "We can talk later if you're busy."

"We can talk now. He's no harm. What did you want to talk about?"

Alden held still. He felt that Grant was using him to put Blodgett on the spot.

Blodgett kept his droopy eyes on Grant and did not bother to look at Alden. "The hell he isn't," he said. "He's cozy with the nesters."

"Pals with the old rat? I doubt it." Grant held his cigarette between his thumb and his second finger and took what Alden perceived as an authoritative drag. He lowered his elbow and blew the smoke straight across the table.

Blodgett went on. "You're the one that wanted to talk about it now, so here it is. We don't like you sidin' with someone else."

Grant's eyebrows went up, and his mouth opened, as if he was making the others wait for what he had to say. He rested his elbow on the table and held his cigarette away from him. "Let me tell you this. I'm not siding with anyone, and you're not telling me what to do. Not you." His eyes shifted to Oates. "Or you." He sat back, and his head lolled an inch to the side. "So put that in your pipe and smoke it."

Blodgett stood up. He was of average height, but he loomed over the table in his black hat and sheepskin coat. A silver watch chain lay across his dark grey wool vest, and the handle of his pistol jutted out in its cross-draw position. With no hurry, he raised his left hand, showing a silver ring with a red stone set in it, and reached into the inside pocket of his coat. He drew out a dull-brown cigar and dropped it on the table in front of Alden. He said, "Here, sonny."

Oates had stood up as well, and the two of them clomped out of the saloon. Alden wrinkled his nose. Blodgett's movements had left a whiff of body odor in the air.

Grant's hand was steady as he raised his glass and took a drink. He pulled one last drag out of the cigarette, dropped the butt on the floor, and ground it with his boot. He said, "Those chumps had better not try anything with me, or they'll wish they hadn't." He leveled his gaze at Alden and nodded.

"I don't know what the cigar is about."

"I think he's trying to rub your nose in something that hasn't happened yet."

"I still don't get it."

"The nester girl. But don't worry. He's not gettin' anywhere. He just thinks he is."

Orval Sledge was chopping wood on the east side of the station house, out of the wind, when Alden rode up. The man was wearing his coarse wool overcoat as usual, and he did not wear a hat or cap. He chopped in an unusual motion, bringing the ax straight down in front of him. When he did so, he bent at the knees. The tails of his coat waved out, and his head of dull brown hair shook. He had his back turned, and Alden decided to bypass a conversation. He tied up his horse and went straight inside.

The Professor sat with his chair tipped back and the heels of his boots on the desktop. With his left hand he held a small book open in his lap. His right hand lay on the edge of the desk, and he held an empty brass rifle casing.

"What have you got there?" asked Alden.

The Professor rolled the casing with his thumb. "Oh, just a little memento from a past time. I suppose I'm something of a magpie." He slipped the casing into his vest pocket.

"I meant the book."

"Oh, this?" He lifted the book, holding it open with his thumb. "It's a slim volume of poetry. Melancholy stuff. Seems to fit this dreary time of year." The Professor sat forward in his chair and put his feet on the floor. "How about yourself?"

"Nothing new. Or not very much. As usual, there seems to be more going on than I'm aware of."

"It doesn't get any better with age, but you won't need me to tell you." The Professor closed the book and set it on his desk. "Something in particular?"

"I'm wondering if you know anything about a couple of characters named Blodgett and Oates."

The Professor shook his head. "Are they from around here?"

"They seem to be at the present. They spend time trying to intimidate the homesteaders out in the Hermit Flats area, and I believe my brother has been riding with them."

"Nothing sounds familiar so far. Except for the Hermit Flats. I think we talked about that area before. It's where Jack Wilcox lives."

"That's right. I know that much, and I've been out there to visit. What I don't know is why these roughnecks are causing trouble or even who they work for."

"Like I say, I don't know. But if I hear something, I'll let you know."

"I'd appreciate it."

"Anything else? How are things out at the Miller place?"

"All right, I suppose. It seems as if I'm going to spend a good part of my time looking for firewood."

The Professor shrugged. "It's not the worst thing to be looking for."

"What is?"

"Gold, which you never find, and trouble, which you always find whether you're looking or not." The Professor smiled, showing his even set of teeth. "But enough wisdom from an older chap. I don't want to deprive you of the joy of discovering these truths for yourself."

"Thank you."

"Thanks to you for the conversation. As I mentioned before, sometimes the substance gets a bit thin around here."

A cold sky was spitting snow as Alden led Miller's two horses to the house. The whole business of looking for deadfall, cutting it up, tying it on, and packing it home was laborious. After all the work, it wouldn't take long to ferry this load into the house. He recalled the old saying that firewood warmed a man twice—once when he cut it, and once when he burned it. In his recent experience, he thought the gathering was out of proportion with the burning, but he was into November now and had to expect periods of being shut in by the weather.

He swung down from Badger and took a couple of trial steps on his cold, stiff legs. A scrap of white caught his eye, a folded slip of paper tucked into the weathered lumber of the door jamb. Without taking off his gloves, he plucked it out, unfolded it, and read the brief contents.

Young friend:
    I think your help is needed. Please pardon the blunt message, but something bad has happened to your brother.
                         Respectfully,
                       Cameron Baker

A heavy wave of dread coursed through Alden's body, stiffening his chest and shoulders. This was what it came to. His brother.

The wind cut sharp and the snow was piling in small drifts as Alden rode into the yard of the bungalow. The chickens had taken shelter, and no horse stood in the corral. Alden dismounted, found his legs, and tied Badger to the hitching rail.

The door opened, showing light in contrast with the greying afternoon. Blond-haired Claudette stood in the doorway and called out.

"I'm so glad you're here."

He hurried across the open space, took care on the steps, and went in. Claudette closed the door and began to cry as she put her arms around him.

"Oh, thank God you came."

He patted her back. "I came here first. The Professor left me a note. I don't even know what happened, though I've got an idea."

With her head still against his coat, she said, "They got him. The dirty sons of bitches, just like he said they were."

Alden released her and drew back. "Where did it happen?"

"Between here and the breaks. Not far from where they left Cash, in fact."

"The same ones?"

She shook her head. "I don't think so. From everything Grant said, the nesters got Cash."

"And his cohorts got him?"

"I don't *know*, but I'm sure that's who did it. He said he had a falling out with them. He said you were there."

"I was."

"Then you know as well as I do."

"I don't know what I know." Fear and agitation ran clear through him. "But I would sure guess those two."

"He didn't take any guff. He said that himself."

Alden let out a long, nervous breath. "And where is he now?"

"In town. They took him to town after they found him. We still have to take care of everything. That's why it's good you're here."

Alden was still trying to take in the magnitude of what had happened. His brother, defiant and pushy but his brother all the same, was no more. Swept away.

Alden tried to think of the right thing to say. "I'm sorry," he began. "Sorry for what happened to Grant, sorry for you, sorry for . . . Florence. One minute he's here, and then . . ." He could not think of the words.

Claudette had tears in her brown eyes, but her face was not wrought up as before. "I thought I saw it coming. I thought I did with Cash, too. Call it my woman's intuition."

Alden was struck by her repose. After her first flurry of emotion, she had become calm, almost matter-of-fact. Now that he thought of it, she had been that way when Cash met his end, also. At first it seemed cold, but Alden realized it must be her way of dealing with adversity and grief. She took refuge in the practical aspects.

Also, he recalled, she had a way of stating things outright, and it often took him by surprise.

He had no sooner made this recollection when she said, "Of course, some of it was your fault, but he wouldn't blame you, and I won't, either."

Alden's stomach tightened. He told himself not to answer. He would have to put up with some remarks. Arguing would not make things any better. He said, "I suppose you'd like to go into town tomorrow."

"Not necessarily. I think you can make the arrangements. I don't know anything about it, and you do. You can come for me and Florence the day of the services."

Alden drove Claudette and Florence back to the bungalow after the funeral. The weak November sun was shining, and the air was cold. Claudette sat next to Alden and held Florence close under a blanket. To Alden, the world and everything in it seemed detached and distant. His brother was in the dark, cold ground, and the men who had done it were free somewhere.

The nervousness that had eaten at him for three days was giving way to a numbness. He did not speak during the whole drive. Perhaps out of consideration for him, Claudette held her silence until he had helped her into the house.

"Don't be in a hurry to leave," she said. "I can start a fire and fix something to eat."

"I'm not hungry."

"You will be. And there's no hurry, anyway. We can talk."

"Talk. I don't know if I'm talked out or just worn out. And I've got to take this buggy back to the livery stable, then check on Miller's place."

"Nothing's going to fall apart. Take off your hat and sit down."

He did, and she took a seat across the table.

"So, what are your plans?" she asked.

"I don't have anything different in mind right now."

She stood up. "I should make some coffee."

"I don't care for any."

"I need to start a fire anyway." She opened the door of the cookstove and began to stuff in some crumpled newspaper. She put slivers of kindling on top, then a few narrow sticks. After lighting the paper and letting the blaze take hold, she stood back and turned so that she was standing about a foot away from him.

He could feel her presence, here in this house where she had lived the life of a woman.

"Don't be afraid to tell me what's on your mind," she said.

"There's not much right now."

She put her hand on his shoulder. "Look," she said. "Life goes on. You can't sit like a bump on a log and let it pass you by."

"I don't think that's what I'm doing, and I don't know what you think I should be doing."

She kept her hand where it was. "We could talk about us."

"Us? My brother is barely in the ground, and you want to talk about us."

"You need to know what you want. He said that himself."

"I'm sure he did."

She squared her shoulders, and her hand went away. "Maybe you don't want me, after all this time."

"I won't say that I do or that I don't."

"You're like the cat and the goldfish."

"I don't know about that one."

"The cat sits on the edge of the water tank. He wants the fish, but he's afraid to get wet."

"Some people put goldfish in their horse troughs. Then the water freezes solid in the winter, and that's it for the goldfish."

"We're talking about the cat, not the goldfish. You know, you."

"Well, I don't think it describes me very well."

"Sometimes a woman knows a man better than he knows himself."

Alden shrugged.

She moved her upper body again. "It's all right. I don't know if I would accept you at this point even if you offered."

Alden took a long breath. He thought it was her way of saying she would, but again he did not answer.

She continued by saying, "I was always second-best with you, anyway."

"I don't know what you mean by that."

Her bosom went up and down as she gave a small huff. "The one they call the nester girl. What does she have that I don't? Or maybe I should say, what does she give you that I didn't? Did you hold that against me? Well, it wouldn't be the same now, because I'm not saving anything."

His temper rose at the way she spoke of Bonnie, and he felt he had been polite long enough. He said, "I suppose Worthington will come around again."

Unfazed, she said, "Don't think I've got any interest in him. Not after what he's done."

A moment of illumination came to him with the image of Blodgett and Oates riding along the road near Silver Springs. "So that's who's behind it," he said. "Harassing the nesters."

"And don't ask me why. I don't think his own men know."

Alden said, "I'd like to find out."

"It won't bring anyone back."

Her eyes met his, and the fire of a couple of minutes earlier seemed to have gone out. Alden felt relief that she did not return to the topic of the two of them. He had the indefinite feeling, which he had had a couple of times before, that she did not see him as a perfect match but did not want to give him up as an option.

He told himself he had to keep his eye on the larger picture. He needed to make sense of what had happened to his brother, he needed to help Claudette if he could, and he needed to keep himself out of danger. Claudette was being flighty right now because of what she had been through. He needed to be willing to let things go and not argue. He could do that as long as she didn't make sharp-tongued comments about Bonnie.

CHAPTER TEN

Badger stood still as Alden brushed him, first with short sweeps and then with long ones. Miller's two sorrels stood a few yards away and watched. The company of horses was comforting on a day like this, with clouds and a chilling breeze and a vast, empty feeling about life. Here he was, Alden Clare, on his feet and alive, with warmth running through him beneath his jacket, gloves, trousers, hat, and boots. The horse he touched was warm and steady. At the same time, miles away, his brother lay in the cold ground, never to see or feel any of this again.

Even if Grant had bullied him in small ways through the years, and even if Grant had talked down to him when they were both on their own, he was his brother. Although Grant had turned his back on his family and had come and gone as he pleased, he had meant it when he said he looked out for his younger brother. Grant might have made his money in questionable ways, in Cheyenne as well as here, and he had belittled the way of life that Alden held dear, but he was still his brother. Now he was gone, and Alden felt an emptiness bigger than he had felt before.

He recalled a scene he had envisioned earlier, a moment in which his father stood by and watched his two little boys eating. Take away the bitterness, take away the misery, and at least they had had a family. Now everything else was gone—his father, his brother, and the place that had been their home. And here he was, set down for the time being by himself, making ten dollars a month, looking after a flimsy homestead that the owner had left to its chances.

Alden put his arms around Badger's neck and laid the side of his head against the horse's jaw. Badger breathed out, soft and peaceful. Alden felt he could let go, miles from anyone and with only two other horses looking on, but not a tear came. His throat felt tight, his nose was congested, and his mouth was dry. He took a long, slow breath, then patted his horse and went back to brushing.

Castle Butte came into view, rising from the plain, steadfast as always. The day remained austere, overcast with a sharp, cold breeze. After riding Badger for a few miles and thinking ahead to the prospect of seeing Bonnie, Alden felt as if he had pulled himself together. His congestion had faded away, and his breathing came easy. His eyes watered a little in the cold air, but his vision was clear. When he held out his hand, his fingers were steady.

Loose weeds and now and then a tumbleweed blew across his path. The land followed a gradual downward slope, and Castle Butte receded from view. A lone jackrabbit with black tips on its ears bolted from sparse cover and ran straight for a quarter-mile until it cut to the right and disappeared over a low rise.

Badger covered the distance at a brisk pace. The sun had climbed in the sky, and weak sunlight was breaking through, when Alden caught sight of the Wilcox homestead. He slowed Badger to a walk and ambled in.

Smoke was trailing out of the stovepipe and drifting on the cross-breeze. As before, Alden tried to decide whether to call out or knock on the door. He dreaded the possibility of being sent away without seeing Bonnie. Still uncertain, he brought Badger to a halt and dismounted.

A small, short-haired, brown-and-black dog came around the corner of the house and began barking. A few seconds later, Bonnie appeared. As on two earlier occasions, she was wearing her customary overalls and wool overcoat. She spoke to the dog and leaned over. The dog quieted down and ran to her, wagging its hind end like a puppy. Bonnie picked up the dog, gave a toss of her dark hair, and smiled.

"Nice to see you again."

"Glad to be able to make it." Alden glanced at the house and spoke in a low voice. "Can you visit today?"

She answered, also in a low tone. "Paul Sherwood is here, and the two of them are having coffee. I think I can talk for a while, though Sooters is likely to come out at any time. This is his dog. Why don't we walk over to this side, where we'll be out of the wind?"

Alden followed her around the corner to the side of the house that faced south, where Bonnie, her father, and Sherwood had sat in attendance as Sooters skinned an antelope. With no chairs present today, Alden stood with reins in hand, facing Bonnie as she held the dog and smiled.

"How have you been?" she asked.

"Not so well the last few days. I don't know if you've heard, but my brother was found dead. Shot."

Her face showed pain. "We heard something, but it wasn't very clear or certain."

"Well, it happened."

"I'm sorry for you."

"Thanks. There's not much to be done about it now."

"Do you have an idea who was behind it?"

"Seems to me, and to others, that it was the bunch he rode with."

Bonnie frowned. "Why would they do that?"

"They had a falling out, partly over me, I guess. But the main thing, as I see it, is that Grant talked back to them—in a rough way. I was there at the time. And not long afterwards, someone found him."

"That's terrible. I'm so sorry for you." She winced at the same time that she patted the dog.

"I appreciate it."

"Isn't there anything anyone can do?"

"It seems to take forever to get a deputy sheriff to come and look into something like this. If it were someone more prominent, they might send a man sooner."

"But they'll send someone?"

"They should, sooner or later. In the meanwhile, if only for my own good, I'd like to know why this bunch is carrying on this vendetta to begin with."

Bonnie shook her head. "I've never gotten a clear reason, beyond what you and I have already talked about."

"There's got to be something more, for people to get killed over it. By the way, I did come across one point of interest, to put it mildly."

"What's that?"

Alden took care as he chose his words. "I was told that some people believe that Cash McGinley received his fatal wounds out this way, maybe at the hands of people who live here."

Bonnie looked over her shoulder. "I don't know. People don't say definite things like that in front of me. But I think it could be true."

Alden shrugged. "Maybe we'll find out, and maybe we won't. Same with Grant. But all of this leaves people's lives in turmoil, not to mention the loss of life to begin with."

"I know what you mean. Both of those boys had families."

Alden felt as if he had a small breath knocked out of him. "There's more to it than you might know. Cash was living with a girl, and they had just had a baby."

"Oh, my. I didn't know that."

"And my brother, Grant, was with the same girl, looking after her and the baby, when he came to an end. I mentioned this girl, Claudette, the last time I was here, but you said you didn't know anything about her, so I left it at that."

Bonnie raised her hand to her mouth. "I had no idea. The poor girl."

"She's had it rough, that's for sure. Though I have to say, she had some part in it. Having the baby, I mean."

"Well, yes."

"I have a hard time getting over that part." He hesitated. "I hope I don't sound heartless after what's happened, but I have a strong feeling against having babies too soon."

Bonnie looked down at the dog as she patted it. "Well, I agree with you on that. I've seen hardship come from it, too." She looked up.

His eyes met hers. He felt encouraged by their mutual understanding, so he forged ahead. "It's nice to know we agree. It seems to me that there's time enough for those things, once a person, or a couple, I should say, gets settled and has something stable."

"It only makes sense."

He laughed. "If everyone followed good judgment all the time—"

She gave a short laugh in return. "Well, yes. People can still be impulsive." She leaned toward him and kissed him on the cheek before he knew it.

He felt himself blushing. "Now, that's nice. I agree with that." He moved toward her, with Badger trailing. He leaned across the dog and kissed her quick on the lips.

She blinked as she regained her posture. "Back to the other part," she said. "About getting settled and being stable. I think that's important. Two people have their house in order, have the things they need, and they can be ready."

He felt a glow, a warm feeling of being in harmony. "That's it," he said. "They have their own home. Not only the things they need, like pots and pans, but maybe something they've always thought of as being part of their own home. Is there something you've always thought of in that way?"

"A sewing machine. My mother had one, but it went by the way." Bonnie's dark eyes were shining. "How about you?"

"I've always thought that having a bookcase would be part of having a home of my own."

"A bookcase? You like to read, don't you?"

"Yes, I do."

"So do I, though I don't get to read much. What kinds of things do you read?"

"*The Courtship of Miles Standish.* Ha-ha. That's a joke. I read it quite a while back. More recently I've read *Great Expectations,* and now I'm reading *Silas Marner.*"

"Oh, I love it. Books are so . . . solid. Or stable, like you said earlier."

"That's how I feel. They keep higher ideas in a safe place, where we can go and . . . participate. I've known people who burn books, but you can always find another copy."

A rough voice broke the charm of the moment. "That's all nice and sweet."

Alden looked past Bonnie and saw the weathered features and dusty black hat of Jack Wilcox. Alden wondered how long the man had been listening.

Jack's dark eyes glinted with resentment. "I'll tell you both, readin' a book doesn't put spuds on the table." He turned to look straight at Alden. "Makes me wonder what kind of a man you are, lyin' on a couch with a perfumed handkerchief, readin' about princes and princesses and fairy godmothers. Hide from real life, 'fraid to look it in the eye."

"That's not the kind of book I read, but—"

"Don't talk back to me. I'd rather you leave right now."

Alden's heart sank. His mouth had gone dry, but he found words. "I'll respect what you say, because this is your place and your daughter."

"You're damned right it is."

"But one of the reasons I came was to ask a question."

"Well, the answer is no."

"It's not a yes-no question."

Jack's eyes narrowed beneath his dark brows. "What is it, then?"

"I'm wondering why Cliff Worthington is carrying on a campaign of harassing you people out here on the Hermit Flats."

Spit flew as Jack said, "What the hell business is it of yours?"

Alden kept a hold of himself. "I believe it caused my brother to come to an early death."

"That's no concern of mine. And as for you, I'd just as soon you were gone. And don't come back. I don't like people snooping, and especially you. Trouble follows you everywhere you go."

Alden held on and tried to keep his voice from shaking. "I'm not snooping, and I didn't cause the trouble. I think I have a right to try to find out what kind of trouble my brother was caught up in."

"Just go. Get the hell gone." Jack's voice had a threatening tone.

"As you wish." Alden took off his hat, made a half-bow toward Bonnie, and turned away.

Behind him, Jack said, "Put that dog down and get in the house."

Alden put on his hat as he led Badger out into the wind and onto the bleak grassland that stretched away for miles.

★　★　★　★　★

A cold wind blew from the northwest, not forceful, but enough to make Alden's eyes water. Riding Badger and leading the stouter of the two horses in his care, he scanned the landscape for the first sign of trees. The grassland rolled away in a mixture of drab grey and tan and faint undertones of green. Tree branches sticking up would be darker, skeletal now in the leafless time of year. Alden was still becoming familiar with this part of the range, so he did not know where the watercourses and scattered draws might hold trees and their deadfall.

At the same time that he kept a lookout for branches, he kept his eyes open for another kind of dark form. Where there were trees, a fellow sometimes saw deer. A haunch of venison would help out, saving him money and bringing a welcome variety from salt pork. The prospect of sizzling red meat lifted his spirits on this dull day.

Far from town and the necessity to pay for supplies, he could forget about money from time to time, but the thought always came back. He owed for his brother's burial. He felt an obligation to help Claudette, who was some version of his brother's widow. He had his own necessities to pay for, try as he might to keep them at a minimum. And he had the always-looming hope, which often felt like a debt itself, of buying back the land that his family had lost. All of that, and he was making ten dollars a month.

When he brushed away the pressing thoughts about money, images of Jack Wilcox came around. Alden felt that he had stood up to Jack as well as he could, but he was no match for the man's hard, menacing way. He had ridden away defeated, demoralized, and when he had held out his hand in front of him, it trembled. He was steady now, but he could not dispel his sense of how forceful Jack Wilcox was at keeping outsiders out.

Alden transferred his reins to his right hand, where he also held the lead rope for the sorrel horse. Reaching down with his left, he touched the stock of his rifle. He rehearsed the motions he would go through if he saw a deer.

Time passed as the sun made its slow climb. As on so many days of late, the sky was hazy and overcast as the cold wind blew at ground level. No trees presented themselves. He decided to change direction, heading north into rangeland even less familiar.

The wind came at him now from the left side. He tipped his head against it but still kept an eye on the country around him. After another mile of riding, in a place that seemed as random as could be, his senses registered something that made him stop the horses.

Beyond the crest of a low hill, at a distance of four hundred yards across a dip in the land, a small group of antelope sat in the lee of a hillside. Alden ducked. He did not think he had shown more than the top of his head, and he did not think the horses had come into view at all. Holding the lead rope out of the way, he slid off the saddle and touched ground.

He led the two horses downhill as he tried to keep his thoughts in order. He needed to be closer to the antelope, and he couldn't let the horses follow him.

At the bottom of the hill, he tied the sorrel's lead rope to the saddle horn on Badger. The sorrel was a placid animal, but Alden did not know what it would do at the sound of a gunshot. He thought he should hobble one of the two horses, so he took off his belt and wound it around the front ankles of the sorrel. With a sense of time pressing, he knotted his reins, flipped them over Badger's head to rest on his neck, and pulled the rifle from its scabbard.

Up the slope again, he took off his hat as he approached the crest. He inched forward until the other hillside came into view.

The antelope sat as before, three of them, sheltered from the wind and taking in the faint sunshine. He needed to move closer, and even if he did, they offered a difficult target when they were bedded down.

Back down the hill a few steps so he could stay well out of sight, he moved to his left. He did not know how much distance he could cut off that way, but he would try.

After going about two hundred yards, he crept to the top again. The antelope were closer, but he still did not have an easy shot. If he went much farther, though, the shape of the land would close them off.

He stalked another hundred yards, took off his coat, and climbed again. He could still see the animals, and he figured this was the best shot he was going to have. Kneeling, he folded his coat and set it on the ground in front of him. Advancing on his knees, he moved it ahead of him until he reached the crest. When he had it in place to cushion his shot, he stretched out into a prone position, shifted his rifle onto the folded coat, and drew a bead.

The animals looked up—not at him, but off to his right. Following their gaze, he saw the sorrel horse galumphing in his direction. The horse was tossing its head to keep the lead rope aside, and it was moving its two front feet together.

The three antelope stood up. The one that offered the clearest shot was a buck with dark horns rising an inch above its ears.

Alden pulled the rifle snug and steadied his aim, and when everything fell into place, he fired. The buck antelope lurched forward in a blur of tan and red, ran twenty yards, and spilled over. Alden levered in another shell and waited. The animal kicked in the air, showing its white underside, and went still.

Alden kept his eye on the antelope until he was sure it was done for. Then he looked around for the sorrel horse. It must have turned and tried to bolt, for it was lying on the hillside and struggling to its feet. With one antelope and two horses to keep track of, Alden had to think fast. He put on his coat, hustled down the hill, laid hold of Badger, and stowed the rifle in the scabbard. A bit shaky from the excitement he had just been through, he decided to walk rather than try to mount up. He leaned forward and tugged on the reins as he climbed the hill, leading Badger.

The sorrel horse was standing still with dust and bits of grass on its hip and in its mane. Alden had fitted the horse that morning with a regular riding saddle, as he had no pack saddle and needed something for tying on a load. He had planned for firewood, but now he would be packing a carcass.

Alden kept hold of the lead rope as he took off the makeshift hobble. With things in order, he led the two horses over the rise and down across the low ground toward the spot where the antelope had died. The tan-and-white body was right where it should be. A red splotch showed where one good shot had put meat on the ground.

With the ropes he had brought to tie on the load of firewood, Alden tethered the two horses to clumps of sagebrush. He took off his coat and tied it to the back of his saddle. Now the work began. Remembering Sooters as well as what he himself knew about antelope, he decided to skin the animal first and then gut it. He was going to have to skin it on the ground, tipping it to one side and another and trying to keep it from picking up dirt and grass, and then he would have to roll out the innards and drain the blood. He took a deep breath and summoned his energy. At least the cold wind would cool the meat. Recalling how soon the sun went down at this time of year, he went to work beneath the vast grey sky.

Alden hung the antelope from the bare rafters in the back room of the homesteader shack. With all the flies dead for the season, he did not have to cover the meat. What little heat came from the kitchen stove did not spread to the back room. He looked over the carcass. An antelope was smaller than a deer, and this one would keep well, but he still had enough to share.

When he checked on the meat the next morning, it was firm and cold. After a breakfast of fried potatoes and antelope tenderloin, he sat near the stove, drank a cup of coffee, and took stock of his situation. The firewood supply was dwindling. His first meager payday was still a couple of weeks away. He was rich in antelope and poor in everything else.

He drank a second cup of coffee as he went to work on the carcass. He cut away one shoulder and hung it separately, then trimmed out the loin all the way down one side of the spine. Next he separated one hindquarter at the hip joint, and laying it on the kitchen table, he took out the leg bone and the thigh bone in one hinged piece. He saw no need to carry the extra weight. The backstrap and hindquarter, even without bones, would amount to an additional fifteen pounds for Badger. The rifle and scabbard could stay at the shack. They added up to another ten pounds and threw the weight off to one side anyway.

He had a full day ahead of him as he mapped it out—one stop at the Professor's, one stop at Claudette's, drop in at the bank before it closed, and try to make it home by dark. Tomorrow he would try again for firewood.

On his way to the bungalow, having left off the antelope loin with the Professor, Alden considered the possibility that Claudette had gone back to stay with her family. When the small house came into view, however, a thin stream of smoke from the stovepipe told him the place was not vacant. Closer, he saw the reddish-brown chickens pecking in the corral, which, to his relief, was otherwise empty.

He rode up to the hitching rail, called out, and dismounted. The door opened as he tied Badger's reins to the rail.

Claudette appeared, wearing a dark grey wool coat of her own and a pair of striped wool pants that had belonged to Grant. She raised her hand to touch her hair, and putting on a smile, she said, "Hello. I didn't know when I'd see you again."

"I brought you some meat." He patted the bundle he had tied onto the back of the saddle.

"I could use it. Did you get a deer again?"

"Antelope. I'd rather have deer, but this is what I found. I hope you don't have anything against it."

"Beggars can't be choosers."

Alden did not answer. He untied the leather strings and hefted the cold chunk of meat.

Claudette stood aside as he carried the bundle up the steps and into the house. He set it on the table and unfolded the cloth he had used to wrap it.

"That's quite a bit," she said.

"You could make some of it into jerky. Hindquarter's good for that. By itself, you might get tired of the taste."

"I'll find a use for it. There's a lot of it, and all meat."

"I could have brought you a jackrabbit."

"We ate that on the farm, too. It's not chicken."

"I see yours are still pecking around."

"I might have had you kill one for me," she said. "But with this meat, I can put it off. Make them last a little longer." She brushed her hand at her hair again. "So, what's new?"

"Nothing to speak of. I'm taking care of this fellow's place, you know. Firewood is pretty scarce out there, so that's the next thing I have to do. How are you fixed for wood?"

"Oh, I'm all right. Grant ordered in a load before he . . . well

. . . you know."

"Uh-huh." Alden wondered if Grant paid for the firewood or if that would be another bill to take care of. "How about other things?" he asked. "I don't mean to be inquisitive, but are you out of money?"

"Pretty close. I can hold out a little longer."

"Do you have an idea what you'll do then? Again, I'm not prying. But if you need some help, I'll see what I can do."

"It's cold in here," she said. She turned and walked to the kitchen stove, where she opened the door on a bright bed of embers. She took a couple of stove lengths from the woodbox, tossed them onto the coals, and closed the door. Returning to stand near Alden, she said, "I didn't know if I wanted to tell you this, but I think I'd better."

He frowned. "Tell me what?"

"Cliff Worthington has been coming around."

Alden's stomach kicked as his pulse went up. "What for?"

Her eyes did not meet his. "Well, me, of course."

"I thought you didn't want to have anything to do with him."

"I don't. But he still comes around."

"There's not much I can do about that."

"You mean you don't want to."

Alden felt as if everything had come to a dead stop. They were right back where they were before he decided to hold his tongue, but he found himself shaking his head.

Claudette went on. "I think it's pointless for you to be living way off over there, and me living here, when we could be in one place, saving time and money and everything else."

He took a deep breath and tried to keep himself calm.

She continued. "But you don't want to. You've told me that." She turned her back to him and moved to the stove, where she held out her palms toward the firebox. "It's warming up," she said. She took off the wool coat, draped it on the back of a chair, and walked with a bit of motion toward Alden. She was wearing a dark-blue sweater that showed her upper body to advantage. As she stood close to him, she gave her blond hair a toss and squared her shoulders. "I wonder if, deep down, you do want to."

His pulse mounted again, and he felt himself on the brink. With the prospect of a long winter ahead in a frigid shack, and with the sting of Jack Wilcox's banishment still smarting, he almost weakened. But he held on. With another small shake of the head, he said, "I just can't."

"You mean you won't."

"Say it how you want to."

"Maybe your brother was right. You wouldn't know what to do with it if it was staring you in the face." She flexed her shoulders as before.

"Don't be so sure."

Now she erupted. "Just like I said before. I knew it. I've never been anything but second-best to you. At one time I thought you were sweet on Julia Redwine, like a silly little puppy, but now I know what it is I'm second-best to. A nester girl."

Alden bore down hard on himself to keep from saying something strong in return. After a long moment he took a steady breath and said, "Look. We're supposed to be friends. You don't know when you're going to need my help."

She still had fire in her eye, though her voice was more subdued. "Maybe you would know what to do. But it just makes me wonder if you'll ever do anything."

He felt drawn toward her. He was convinced he could have done something, just this once, and still gotten away. But he let the moment pass. His mouth was dry, and he moistened it. "I'll check back with you again in a few days," he said. "If you need something, don't be afraid to ask. I've got a little money in the bank, and I'm planning to take out some of it."

She spoke in a neutral tone. "Thanks. And thanks also for the antelope meat. It'll help."

A minute later, he was in the saddle, waving goodbye and turning Badger around. As he settled in for the ride back to town, he let out a long breath of relief. He felt as if he had been on the bank of a swift river, wide and smooth, where riders and their horses were rolled over and carried away in the current while cattle, with eyes and noses sticking out of the water, were also pulled under. He had been on the edge, and even now, his hand trembled.

CHAPTER ELEVEN

The teller with the slicked-back hair, wire-rimmed spectacles, and clipped greying mustache raised his head in a slow motion and looked down his pointed nose at Alden.

"Yes?"

"I would like to withdraw some money from my account."

"Your name?"

Alden took in a measured breath. He had expected the man to condescend to him in some way. Alden had opened his account less than a month earlier, and he was sure the teller remembered not only his name but the amount he had deposited. "Alden Clare," he said.

"I see. And how much would you like to withdraw?"

Alden had given the amount plenty of thought, and it pained him to say, "Twenty dollars."

"Just a minute. I'll have to check the balance." The teller stepped aside, thumbed through a ledger, paused, and turned back toward the window grate with a somber expression. "Any particular way you'd like it?"

"Two five-dollar gold pieces and ten silver dollars, if it's not too much trouble."

The teller gave him a withdrawal slip to sign. Then he stacked the coins and pushed them beneath the grate toward Alden as if they were poker chips. "Here you go. Anything else today?"

"No, thank you. That's all." Alden took the coins from the counter. As he stepped away from the teller window, he craned his neck to catch sight of Mr. Newton Dorrance.

The banker's bushy white mustache was barely visible as he kept his shiny head fixed downward. Alden waited a few seconds to see if the man would look up, but he didn't. Alden had the impression, though it was only a feeling, that the banker would rather not have any contact with him. Alden recalled the embarrassment he had felt after their last meeting, when he thought he had tried too hard to ingratiate himself with the banker, and he wondered if Mr. Dorrance was giving him the cold shoulder to avoid any similar encounter now.

The teller, also, paid him no further attention as he took one last look at the cage-like window, the desks, the vault, and the banker's sanctuary. Alden's bootheels sounded on the wooden floor as he walked to the door.

Outside once again, he glanced at the sky. The sun was slipping in the southwest, not quite at the point where it made the fast plunge to sunset. The air was not warm at the moment, and it would turn colder on his ride back to the Miller homestead.

Halfway down the next block, the Professor stepped out of Julia Redwine's store. He lifted his head in recognition and picked up his pace as he walked toward Alden.

Badger snuffled. Alden untied the reins and patted the horse on the neck, then turned and waited for the Professor to arrive.

"Young Nimrod," said the Professor, cheery as ever.

"Good afternoon. What's new?"

"Nothing since I saw you last. Except that I fried up some of that antelope loin you gave me. Mighty fine. I shared it with my man Friday. He approved."

Alden smiled at the thought of Orval Sledge being a connoisseur of frontier cuisine. "That's good."

"And yourself? Homeward bound?"

"That's right. If I don't lose any time, I should get there by dark."

"I won't keep you, then. I didn't ask earlier, but I trust that everything is all right there."

Alden shrugged. "Not much to it. I'm running low on firewood, and I have to go a ways to find some. I think I might try Castle Butte. I'll have to climb a ways, but as I recall, I've seen dead stuff on the sides."

"Reminds me of New Mexico. In some places down there, they say they have to climb for water and dig for wood."

Alden frowned and gave a questioning look.

"They find water where it collects in hollowed-out tanks in the rocks, what they call *tinajas*. And they dig up roots of things like ironwood and mesquite, after someone else has taken the dead growth from above ground. Hard country there. Not that it's easy here."

"Maybe I'll visit there someday."

"Go in the good time of year."

"When's that?"

"A little earlier than here. Between the twentieth and the twenty-fifth of March. No sooner and no later." The Professor took a pair of leather gloves from his coat pocket and began to put them on. "Starting to get cold. I'd better not keep you any longer. I can see that you're booted and spurred and ready to ride."

Alden smiled as he recognized the line. "Like Paul Revere."

"Good lad," said the Professor. He touched the brim of his hat. "Take care of yourself."

Snippets of "Paul Revere's Ride" were still running through Alden's head the next morning as he climbed the frosty slope of Castle Butte. He found wood to his liking, especially cedar, but for every piece that was big enough to bother with, he had to cut off a multitude of small tough branches up to an inch thick. By midday he had sixteen pieces ranging from three to four feet long and one to four inches thick. He estimated the total weight at about two hundred pounds, as much as he thought he should put on the sorrel horse. Tying on the load promised to be a chore in itself, and he would still have to cut the wood into stove lengths when he had it in the yard. This supply was going to warm him twice in the gathering and cutting and once in the burning. He was going to appreciate every glowing ember.

Alden opened and closed his hands as he rode Badger across the open country. After two days of cutting wood, with the ax handle finding new places to pinch the skin after breaking old calluses, his hands grew stiff. The gloves helped, but the air was cold, and his hands did not move much when he was riding.

His upper body tensed with the cold as well. He flexed his chest and abdominal muscles and relaxed, and he could feel a bit of warmth circulating. At the same time, he could not dispel his sense of dread, or apprehension. He had told Claudette he would check in on her in a couple of days, and he stayed good on his word, but he did not know what to expect. Now that he thought of it, there was one thing he could expect—conflict— but he could not guess in what form it would present itself.

As he approached the bungalow, the chickens were scratching as usual in the corral and in the yard. A wisp of smoke rose from the stovepipe. A curtain moved at the window, and a half-minute later, the door opened.

Claudette appeared, dressed as before in a wool overcoat and wool pants. She put her hands in her coat pockets and squinted at the daylight. "Good to see you again."

Alden swung down from the saddle and tied the reins at the rail. "I said I'd come back in a couple of days, so I did."

"I haven't made any jerky yet, but I've fried up some of the meat, and it's been good."

"Glad to hear it."

"Come in," she said. "Florence is asleep, and I'm trying to get a couple of things done."

He followed her into the dim house. The interior was warm, at least in comparison with the day outside. A stale odor, perhaps of baby laundry, hung in the air.

"I could make some coffee," she said. She smoothed her blond hair with her hand.

"Don't go to the bother. I don't care for any right now." After a pause, he said, "Anything new to report?"

"Not here, and I haven't been anywhere else."

He took off his gloves and reached into his coat pocket. "I brought you some money. Not much, but I hope it helps." He handed her a five-dollar gold piece and five silver dollars.

"Thanks," she said. She let her brown eyes meet his. "You don't have to, you know."

"Yes, I know. But I thought it would be the right thing to do. I know we don't agree on things, but we're friends, and we're family, in a way—at least in the sense that my brother left you in these circumstances."

"I'm not expecting, if that's what you're hinting at."

He almost coughed, taken off guard as he was by her directness. "I wasn't thinking in that way, though I suppose it's good to know."

"Well, I thank you all the same. It'll help. Though I don't know how I'll get to town."

Alden hesitated. "I suppose I could get a buggy."

"Maybe I should give you back the money until then."

He sighed. "Let's just leave things the way they are for the time being. I'll see what I can do. I wasn't thinking that far ahead, and I haven't wanted to ask whether you have anyone else to help you do things."

"If you mean Cliff Worthington, no. He comes around, but I keep telling him no."

Alden had the sense, which he had not quite recognized to himself earlier, that she was trying to use Worthington as a way of making him jealous. He decided not to take the bait, if that was what it was. He asked, "Has he been here since I dropped in the other day?"

"Once."

Alden shrugged. "You must not be telling him very well."

"I tell you, I'm not doing anything with him."

"Not now."

Claudette gave a small huff. "If you must know, I did once. And only once. That was before Grant and I were together. But not since then. Not at all."

Alden thought back, and he had an idea of when the one time might have been. He recalled meeting Worthington on the trail not far from the bungalow. "Well," he said, "None of that is my business. I've probably said more than I should already."

"It doesn't matter."

"We'll leave it at that." After a pause, he said. "I'll tell you what. I'll see about getting you to town so you can shop for a few things you need."

"Thanks. I appreciate it."

As Alden rode away a short while later, he thought back on the conversation. He widened his eyes and shook his head as he recalled how forward Claudette was with some of the things she said. Then there was the casual manner of brushing things away with "It doesn't matter."

He almost coughed again as another breath went out of him. Maybe she meant something when she said it didn't matter. After all, she had accepted Alden's money, and if she had been doing something with Worthington, or if she had been expecting from either him or Grant, it would indeed have mattered.

Perhaps what she meant was that earlier actions didn't matter if there were no current consequences.

By the time he had covered half the distance from the bungalow to town, Alden had his thoughts collected. He felt as if he was caught up on everything that had been pressing him. He had meat and firewood at the shack. He had paid his brother's burial on the way through town that morning, and he had given Claudette some money to help her get by. He would have a dab of money coming in. The sky was even a little brighter, as the clouds and haze had cleared away. A clear sky made for colder nights, but the sun felt warmer than it had felt for several days.

One big item, however, was not so bright and sunny. When he let himself think about it, Alden felt Jack Wilcox's orders hang like a pall over him. Alden was sure that Bonnie's feelings had not changed any more than his own had, but he could not yet imagine how they were going to maneuver around her father's pronouncement.

At least Claudette had not said anything about Bonnie. Not this time.

The only thing working against them was her father. That was all. They needed to move past that. If only he could see her—he was sure she felt the same way as he did.

He wondered about the power of thought. If he wanted to see her, and if she wanted to see him, was there some way their thoughts would meet and direct them to the same place? He imagined it could be so. If he rode to the Hermit Flats, a feeling, or a higher power, might tell him where to linger, and it might tell her as well. What a stirring thought it was, this idea of fate or destiny that would help them be together.

That was what he needed to do—go to the Hermit Flats and follow the feeling he had. Something above—the sun or the moon or a spirit—would relay their signals like a telegraph code. In some way, she would know to look for him, and he would be there to be found.

And when they met, the scene would be simple and pure. Like John Alden in the poem, he would "not embellish the theme, or array it in beautiful phrases." They would join in their certainty that they were meant for one another. Sooner or later, her father, like gruff old Miles Standish, would accept the inevitable. Love would conquer all.

Badger hit one hoof against another, as he sometimes did, and the small jarring brought Alden down from his cloud. He recognized that he might ride to the Hermit Flats, watch the night close in around him, and ride home in the frigid night. But he was willing to try to catch a few minutes with Bonnie.

A sense of mundane reality set in as Alden drew closer to the Hermit Flats. The idea that he might communicate with Bonnie through some kind of telepathy began to seem naive at best. He told himself that if he was going to meet up with her at all, he was going to have to present himself within view of her house, which meant that her father might see him as soon as she would. He shrugged. He had come this far. He was going to have to risk it.

By his estimate, he had less than a mile to go until the Wilcox homestead would come into view. Many of these grassy hills looked the same, and sometimes there were more than he expected, but he had a general familiarity with the layout of this area, and he thought he would see something before long.

With that expectation, he was surprised to see instead a couple of riders emerge from the landscape. They seemed to rise out of the ground, much closer and bigger than in his usual experience. The men were thirty yards away and approaching. Alden focused on the details.

The man on his left wore a brown hat and a coarse wool

overcoat of a nondescript grey. He rode a slender bay horse with a thin mane and no white markings.

The man on Alden's right wore a dull black hat, a sheepskin coat, and batwing chaps. He had a rough-looking face with a week's stubble. His horse was of a medium shade of brown, all one color, with no black or white markings. When Alden's gaze returned to the man's face, closer now, he recognized the drooping eyelids of Art Blodgett.

A flickering glance at the other man confirmed George Oates with his pointed ears and gapped yellow teeth.

As the two rode forward, they shortened the distance between themselves and Alden, blocking his trail. Alden drew rein, but the men did not stop until their horses' noses were a yard from Badger's.

Alden's heart was beating fast. These were the men he thought were responsible for his brother's death. They had no good intentions.

Blodgett spoke. He was close enough that he did not have to raise his voice. "Off your range a ways, aren't you, sonny?"

Alden did not answer. His view traveled from Blodgett to Oates and back.

"Where do you think you're going?"

"That way." Alden motioned with his head. He did not look at his hand, but he knew it was trembling.

"What for?"

"I'm just on a ride. That's all."

"Well, aren't you tough? It must run in the family."

Alden felt a chill in his blood.

Oates rode forward, turned, and laid his hand on the headstall of Badger's bridle. Badger tried to move his head, and Oates tightened his hold. In a gravelly voice he said, "Don't try anything smart, kid."

Alden's heart was beating faster as Oates edged his horse

around and pushed against Badger.

Blodgett rode forward, pulling the glove off his left hand and holding it by the fingers. Crowding close to Alden, he swung backhanded and slapped Alden's face with the glove. Alden felt the sting, and on the man's bare left hand, he saw the silver ring with the red stone in it. He remembered the ring from the day in the saloon when Blodgett had dropped a cigar on the table in front of him.

Blodgett's face tightened as he swung again and whipped Alden with the gauntlet of his glove. Oates crowded from the other side, holding the headstall firm as Badger jostled.

Blodgett passed the glove to his left hand, and with his right, he took hold of the front of Alden's coat. As he pulled, Alden grabbed his saddle horn. Oates's hand came smashing down, and Alden let go. Blodgett reined his horse around and dragged Alden out of the saddle. Alden felt his boots slipping away from the saddle leather. Blodgett held him dangling for a second, then came around with his left fist clutching the glove as his knuckles and the ring slammed into Alden's cheekbone. Alden's head went back as he felt the impact. Blodgett let go, and Alden fell to the ground.

The horses drew away as Alden came to his feet. Oates was still mounted and kept hold of Badger's headstall. Blodgett's horse was backing away, its saddle empty, as the man in the dusty hat and sheepskin coat blocked out the sun. Blodgett was wearing both gloves again, and he held his arms out as if he was cornering an animal in a corral. Alden did not know which way to move. Blodgett's first swing landed on the left side of Alden's head, knocking him off balance. The other hand caught him square on the right side, stopping him, and Blodgett moved closer. When he hit the third time, his gloved hand was doubled in a fist, and he caught Alden on the temple.

Alden felt the jolt to his head as his feet went out from under him. He heard Blodgett seething, and he smelled his body odor. He thought the man was going to pounce on him like an animal.

But he didn't. He stood over Alden, his fists at his side, and he spoke in a slow, rough voice. "Now get this, sonny. You go home, on foot, and mind your own business. Don't come back. Don't try anything smart. If you do, you'll end up like your brother."

As Blodgett turned to walk away, Alden said, "I want my horse. You can't take someone's horse."

Blodgett turned, rolled his head, and opened his droopy eyes. "Want? You tell me what you want?" Blodgett held his arms open and looked around. "Did you hear that?"

Alden followed his line of sight, and there sat Cliff Worthington, wearing a dark overcoat, atop a dark, unmarked horse. Alden's spirits sank.

Blodgett stood over Alden once again. "Get up, kid."

"So you can knock me down again?"

"I said get up. Don't make me do something worse."

As Alden pushed himself up onto his feet, Blodgett stepped forward and clobbered him on the left ear. Alden hit the ground again, taking a jolt to his shoulder.

"That's just to help you understand, kid, that you don't get what you want. Now it's a long walk home, and I suggest you get started. As you go, get used to that idea. You don't get what you want."

Blodgett stood back and looked at his boss. "What do you think?"

"I don't like him."

"I mean about getting what he wants. I think it's a lesson a boy should learn."

Worthington said, "You make me laugh."

He was looking at Alden but speaking to Blodgett, and there was not a trace of humor in his cold voice.

Chapter Twelve

Twice on his long walk to the Miller homestead, Alden had to stop and pull himself together. The total discouragement and humiliation was too much, and he had to lean forward, resting his forearms on his knees, and take deep breaths. The desperation welled up in him, but he was unable to let go. He had been threatened and beaten, and he had had his horse, his only true companion in a year of troubles, taken from him. He had been left to pick himself up off the ground and trudge away in defeat. He would have cried if he could; he would have sobbed. But he couldn't. All he could do was feel abused and degraded as he set one foot in front of the other. After his second spell, he summoned up enough will to walk the rest of the way in the dark.

Miller's two horses drew close and nudged him. They wanted grain. He gave it to them. He would need them now.

He did not sleep well. He wanted to cry for his horse, for his brother, for his father, even for his mother, whom he barely remembered. But the tears did not come, and his throat remained swollen.

In the morning, as weak daylight struggled through the window, he realized he was breathing easier. His heartbeat had returned to normal, and when he flexed his hands, most of the stiffness had gone away. He remembered opening and closing his hands all the way back from the Hermit Flats, to keep warm and to work off frustration.

A deep pang of sadness ran through him now as he lay in his

bedroll and thought of Badger. He had to get his horse back. He could not bear the idea of having Badger taken away by force and injustice. It was only right for him to have his horse again. But he knew that things did not always turn out right. Baldy, for example, had never showed up again. The horse disappeared when Cash was killed. Alden was sure the horse was gone for good—sold or traded, he imagined. Worthington's gang had no use for horses with white markings. They showed in the dark. Light-colored Badger would not last long in their hands, either.

Resentment and anger began to take the place of yesterday's helplessness and anguish. As he closed his fist, he wanted to punch someone—Blodgett or Worthington or even Oates. Any one of the three could have beaten him up, but they hadn't allowed him a fair fight. If the chance came around now, he would strike.

The same with a gun. They had killed his brother and had threatened to do the same to him. And for what? For siding with a nester girl that Blodgett fancied, and for being on friendly terms with a girl that Worthington would like to lay his hands on again.

For the first time, it occurred to Alden that one of Worthington's motives for doing away with Grant might have come from his desire to have Claudette. The rest of the motive, Alden imagined, had more to do with authority. But beneath it all lay the still unexplained reason why Worthington was tormenting the nesters to begin with.

Alden shivered in his bedroll. These men were ruthless, and he was going to have to stand up to them for his own reasons, even if it meant using a gun.

Alden brushed and saddled the stout sorrel horse. He was used to Miller's horse and did not have any hesitation about riding it, but in his heart he was convinced that Badger was a better horse and that his was a better saddle. He had to take them back. At the same time, he knew that the world at large did not care about his individual plight. As much as he despised Blodgett and his coarse manner, he knew there was some truth in the taunt that a person didn't always get what he wanted.

Alden brought the rifle and scabbard out from the house. He hung the stirrup on the saddle horn and went about buckling the narrow strap that held the front of the scabbard to the "D" ring above it. Next he secured the strap that reached up to the rear "D" ring. The sorrel had a broad belly, so the length of the rifle and scabbard stuck out along the side. Alden didn't plan to ride through any trees, but he still had to keep an eye on the rifle stock.

Focusing on the practical matters was easy. So was stalking a deer or antelope, or shooting at a coyote, compared to what he might have to do in the near future. He had never shot at a man, and he did not want to do so unless he had to. But he was up against some fellows, grown men, who had beaten him, taken his horse and saddle, and killed his brother. They did not play fair, and they had guns.

He ran his hand along the stock of the rifle. If he had to use it, he would.

On his way to the Hermit Flats, Alden varied his approach from the day before. He knew that if Worthington's men were keeping an eye out, they could surprise him anyway, but he did not want to ride past the scene where he had been humiliated. At the same time that he kept himself prepared for a run-in with the hoodlums, he bolstered his nerve for a meeting with Jack Wilcox. If he had to, he was going to defy the man's orders.

Riding up to the homestead, he did not see woodsmoke or any other sign of life about the house. In the corrals in back, the dark head of a cow appeared. Alden saw no horses. He assumed Wilcox still had two, but the wagon sat idle.

Alden decided to try his luck. He had the notion, at the moment, that if he did not speak words, he would not invite words. So he tried a sound he had heard among the cowpunchers.

"Yoodle-oodle-ooh!"

He waited a moment and called again. *"Yoodle-oodle-ooh!"*

The clang of a bucket handle sounded—not in answer, but as if someone had stopped to listen or had set down the bucket to come take a look.

He dismounted and waited with the reins in his hand. At last a motion caught his eye, and his heartbeat jumped at the sight of Bonnie.

She was dressed as usual in her wool overcoat, denim overalls, and brogan shoes. Her hair was tucked under the collar of her coat, and she was squinting in the daylight.

"Alden. You came back."

"I had to." He longed to see her flowing dark hair, to touch her hand or arm, but he heeded the seriousness of the moment.

She shaded her eyes with her hand. "What happened to you?"

He brushed his gloved fingers down the side of his face. "Blodgett and Oates got a hold of me. They beat me up and took my horse."

She looked past him. "Whose horse is that?"

"The fellow whose place I'm looking after."

"Where did it happen?"

"Not too far from here. These fellows are supposed to be working on a ranch over by Silver Springs, but it seems like they spend a lot of time out this way."

"They do. My father says they have a camp over in the breaks. He and Paul Sherwood have gone to spy on it a couple of times. That's where they are now."

Alden nodded. It accounted for the horses being gone. He

said, "I was on my way to see you yesterday when I ran into those thugs. Their boss was there, too, though I didn't see him at first."

Her eyes roved over him. "They roughed you up."

"I felt worse yesterday. Not that I felt very well when I got up this morning. But I had to do something, so I came back." He hesitated. "Has your father said anything about me since the last time I was here?"

"Not a word. He hasn't said much of anything, but when he does talk, he goes on about these ruffians."

"No idea why they keep it up?"

She shook her head. "At one time, I thought they were trying to push us out. But I think they're trying to goad us into doing something."

"Maybe Blodgett has other motives as well."

"If you mean me, he's not going to get very far." She puffed out a little breath. "You would think he would know better, but he seems to think that if he exerts his will enough, he'll get his way."

"At the same time, he's willing to tell others they don't get what they want."

"He told you that?"

"About my horse and saddle. I told him I wanted them back, and he as much as laughed at me."

"Well, you have to get them back."

"I know. I'm just not sure how."

Their conversation was interrupted by popping sounds from the east.

Alden said, "That sounds like rifle shots."

Bonnie frowned. "I hope not."

"Is that the direction where your father and Paul Sherwood went?"

She nodded.

Three more pops sounded.

"I hope it's not trouble," she said.

"We'll see." He turned and peered toward the east. He saw nothing but bare grassland.

Bonnie moved forward to stand beside him. Her face was tensed with worry. "I just hope . . ."

He took her hand and squeezed it.

After a few long minutes of silence, two dots appeared on a rise in the land. A minute later they dipped out of sight; then they appeared again, a little larger. Two men on horseback left a trail of dust. They were not riding at a dead run.

Half a mile away and coming closer, the men were recognizable as Jack Wilcox and Paul Sherwood—Wilcox on the right with his black hat and dark features, and Sherwood on the left, wearing a winter cap and a long coat that flapped like a cape. His horse had a jolting gait, and he was bouncing in the saddle. Wilcox, meanwhile, was leaning forward and seemed to be grabbing the saddle horn with both hands.

Alden and Bonnie waited as the riders went out of sight again and reappeared. When the men were a hundred yards out, Paul Sherwood tumbled from the saddle and rolled on the ground. Wilcox, hunched and grimacing, rode on in.

He did not dismount but sat swaying in the saddle as he leaned forward. His face was pale in contrast with his dark brows and black neckerchief.

Paul Sherwood came running up to the group. Between breaths, he said, "They started farrin' at us fer no reason. We weren't nowhere near their camp. They just farred at us. We come ridin' like the wind. I think yer pa's hurt bad."

Bonnie hurried around to the side of her father's horse.

Paul Sherwood kept talking. "It's been like this all along. They won't leave the little man alone. Poosh and poosh, and now it comes to this."

Bonnie said, "Can I help you down?"

"Get out of the way," Jack said.

Paul Sherwood went on. "Not a reason in the world."

"Did they follow you?" Alden asked.

"I don't know." Sherwood's mouth was open, showing a pink interior with dark spots where teeth were missing.

"I heard two sets of shots. That's why I wonder if they kept after you."

"I guess they did, but I didn't look back to see."

Alden motioned to Bonnie. "If you stand aside, I'll try to help him down."

Alden kept his eye on Jack, expecting him to fall at any moment. In an instant, Jack stiffened, a wide look of pain appeared on his face, and the crash of a rifle shot followed. Blood appeared in the seam of Jack's lips, and he pitched forward, falling from the saddle as his horse bolted away.

Bonnie shrieked, then knelt to tend to her father.

Alden looked past the small group, trying to keep track of the two horses. A couple of hundred yards to the east, a horse disappeared over a low grassy ridge. It was a dark horse, with a rider wearing a dark overcoat. Alden's first thought was of Worthington, but he couldn't be sure.

Bonnie was on her knees, cradling her father's head. "Papa! Papa!" she cried, as her tears fell.

"They finally did it," said Sherwood. "And we weren't doin' a damn thing." He wiped the back of his hand across his nose.

Bonnie looked up, her face ravaged with fear and urgency. "We've got to move him into the house."

Sherwood peered close. "I think he's done for, Bonnie."

"I don't care. We can't leave him here in the dirt. That's his house. We have to get him in there."

"I know. I know." Sherwood walked a few steps away and picked up Jack's hat where it had fallen. He straightened up and sniffled, then returned to stand over his friend. He shook his head as he gazed down. "It's a bum deal. They never gave him a chance."

When they had Jack laid out on the couch, Alden stood a respectable distance from Bonnie and asked, "What would you like me to do?"

Her face was swollen, and her eyes were red. She daubed at her nose with a handkerchief and said, "Someone has to report this, and bring back help if he can."

"I'll go," he said.

Paul Sherwood spoke up. "I'll get Sooters, and the two of us will stay here. I'll put the horses away, too."

Alden turned to Bonnie. "I'm sorry about all of this."

She drew in a breath as she raised her head. "I was afraid all along that something like this would happen, but I didn't want to believe it. Now it's happened, and there's nothing anyone can do about it."

"Nothing to change things, that is."

"Yes, that's what I meant."

"I'll do what I can," he said. "I don't know when I'll be back, but I'll try for tomorrow." He turned to Sherwood, who was staring away at the wall. "Are you sure you'll be all right here?"

Sherwood wiped his moist eyes and blinked a couple of times. "Nothing else we can do. As far as Madge and the other kids go, I think they'll be all right. These outlaws never came by my place. They acted like they wanted to run off all of us, but they always seemed to have it in for Jack."

As Alden rode toward town, veering wide of the breaks, it occurred to him that one person might be able to help him understand more about Worthington. Halfway to town, then, he reined the sorrel to the east and headed toward the bungalow.

Although he thought Worthington and the others would still be holed up in the breaks, he knew he could not count on it. They could be headed back toward their place near Silver Springs, or Worthington himself could be making one more try at Claudette's.

Alden shuddered as he recalled an image that had come to him several times, that of Jack Wilcox stiffening, his face wide in pain, as his assassin shot him in the back. The more Alden thought of the brief view he had had of the retreating dark figure, the more convinced he was that the killer was Cliff Worthington. At the same time, he admitted to himself that he was believing what he wanted to believe. That went for his idea that Worthington was still hanging out in the breaks, also.

Alden took a cautious approach to the bungalow, easing up from the south as he had done with Bill Smith, and taking a view of things from the back of the place. He felt relief at seeing no horses in sight. The reddish-brown chickens picked here and there with their usual calmness.

He rode around to the front and called out as he came to a stop at the hitching rail. He dismounted and waited.

The door scraped open an inch and stopped. A minute later, Claudette appeared, wrapping a grey wool blanket around her shoulders. "Back again," she said. "Good to see you. Come on in."

He tied the reins to the rail, stretched his legs as he walked to the steps, and went up into the house. The interior was warm, and a pleasant odor of scented soap or powder hung in the air.

"I just gave Florence a bath and tucked her away," Claudette said. "Can I offer you something? I've got coffee made."

"I could do with a cup."

She turned her back as she headed for the kitchen. "You look worried. Is there something new?" She unwrapped the blanket and draped it on the back of a kitchen chair. She was wearing her dark-blue wool sweater and a long grey wool skirt.

Alden took a seat at the table. As she drew near with the coffeepot and two cups, he said, "Jack Wilcox has been killed."

She slowed down, set the cups on the table, and poured the coffee. "That's the nester fellow, isn't it?"

"Yes, it is."

"When did this happen?"

"Earlier today. I was there."

She settled her eyes on him. "Does that have anything to do with the marks on your face? It looks like you've been in a fight."

"Well, it's related, in that Worthington's roughnecks beat me up and took my horse. When I went back over that way to see what I could do, I was talking to Bonnie when her father and a neighbor came riding back from some kind of a skirmish. Jack had been shot, and he was slow to climb down from his horse when they stopped in the yard. While he was still sitting in the saddle, someone shot him in the back. I barely got a glimpse, but it looked like Cliff Worthington riding away."

Claudette gave a heavy breath across the top of her coffee cup, clearing the steam. "So it has come to that."

"Yes, it has." He took a sip of coffee. "I have the impression that you've gathered a little knowledge about that situation."

She shrugged. "I've heard a thing or two."

He tried to pick his words with care. "I had thought, before, that you would have heard a few things from Grant, but I've come to think that you might have heard something from Worthington himself. You said you were familiar with him at one time."

She shrugged again. "Only once, like I told you. But I talked to him more than once, of course. I didn't roll in the hay with him the first time."

Alden winced, as he had done before, at her forwardness, but he stayed on course. "One thing I'd like to know, if there's a way to find out, is why he's gone to all the bother of pushing around Jack Wilcox and finally shooting him."

Claudette raised her eyebrows. "It's hard to know everything."

"I know it is. For example, why they did in my brother. Sure, he talked back to them and acted tough with them, but my hunch is that Worthington was jealous of him as well."

Her voice had a tone of resentment as she said, "Don't think that it hasn't occurred to me as well. I have nothing good to say about him or any of his motives, and to tell you the truth, I'm afraid of him. I don't want to have anything to do with him, but he won't take 'No' for an answer. And now with this news about what they did to the nester—well, I just don't know what he'll stop at." She sat up straight, gave her blond hair a slight toss, squared her shoulders one at a time, and showed the dark-blue sweater to advantage. "I was hoping you would help me."

He held onto his resolve. "Maybe I can. But I'd still like to know what Cliff Worthington has against Jack Wilcox. If you know anything, it would help me decide how to proceed."

"Proceed in what?"

"Well, you know I've got to help her if I can. If this fellow is capable of shooting someone in the back, I need to be more than careful, and anything I know will help me."

She seemed to sulk, or at least hesitate, as she bit her lower lip and kept her eyes on her cup. After a moment she looked up, held her brown eyes on him, and said, "I'll tell you what I know."

Alden's heartbeat picked up. He had to be ready for anything. "Go ahead."

"To begin with, Cliff's father and Jack Wilcox, as you call him, were partners. They robbed trains along the U.P. Three in all, I think. Cliff's father got his share of the take in the first two, and he stashed it. Just before he died, in prison, he told

Cliff where it was, and that's how Cliff had the stake to buy the ranch he did. But for the third job, which was the biggest one and the one Frank—Cliff's father—went to prison for, Jack made off with all the money. Frank never peached on him, but he carried the grudge, of course. So did Cliff."

As Alden let the information sink in, he saw the irony of Jack's declaration that reading a book never put spuds on the table. "I suppose it shouldn't surprise me that Jack Wilcox was a train robber," he said, "but if he made off with a good sum of money, you'd think he would buy a better place than a hardscrabble homestead on the Hermit Flats."

"I think he went off and squandered a large part of it. Left his wife and daughter on their own, and came back when he was broke. And as far as that goes, Wilcox isn't his real name. It's Brody. He was known as Black Jack Brody."

Alden let out a long breath. As he was absorbing the information, he understood why Jack did not want anyone getting close or knowing anything. More than once he had expressed his dislike for people snooping. "It's beginning to make sense," he said. "Black Jack Brody. And his partner was Frank Worthington, then?"

"From what I understand, that's not Cliff's original last name, either."

"I think it's common for criminals to take on another name when they go somewhere else and start over."

"I suppose. But I think Cliff took on a new name so Jack wouldn't know who he was."

Alden took another sip of coffee. "That makes sense. He must have a tremendous grudge."

"He does. He hates Black Jack for leaving his father to rot in jail, as he says. Of course his father hated Jack, too, though he never turned witness."

"Why did it take the son so long to get even?"

"To begin with, it took him quite a while to track him down. For Black Jack Brody to turn into a hardscrabble homesteader, as you say, was pretty unlikely. Then, once he found him, I guess he wanted to torment Black Jack, run him into the ground, and then get even. And now he's done it."

"But things aren't finished."

She regarded him with her brown eyes open. "In what way do you mean it?"

"Well, someone has to bring him to justice, if we can ever get a deputy sheriff to come here. Then a smaller matter, but a big one to me, is that they still have my horse and saddle. I can't let them get away with that."

She let out a puff of breath. "Who knows how much of that you may be able to do."

"I know. I'm not taking anything for granted. And then there's one other little thing. This fella Blodgett seems to think he should be able to sidle up to Bonnie. I don't know how he could still think that way after they've killed her father, but I can't count him out."

Claudette shrugged, giving Alden the impression that this latter point did not have great significance to her.

"By the way," he said. "You mentioned that Worthington is not his original name. Do you know what it was?"

Her eyes met his and moved away. "That's one thing I'd rather not say. Any of this could come back on me."

"I realize that. Someone's going to want to know, especially the law, but I'm sure there are ways to find out. A train robber named Frank something who died in prison."

"Sure. I just don't want to be the one to say. I've told you as much as I have, which is almost everything, anyway, because you asked me. Also, I thought that if you knew how much danger Florence and I are in, you would help us. I don't know what he'll do next, but I don't think he'll leave me alone. He seems too determined."

Alden nodded, moving his head to each side as he did so. He was going to have to form a plan. Right now his obligations were too spread out between Miller's place, Bonnie's place, and here.

Claudette shifted in her seat. "Look," she said. "I know we've said little things and had little disagreements. I'd like to leave it all in the past."

"I think we've agreed that we're friends and should help each other, and maybe we've said things since then. So your suggestion is fine with me. I'm just trying to think of a way to do things."

"Don't take too long."

For a second he felt as if he was in the past, with her pushing him like always, but he let it go. "I won't. But I need to go to town first, to report Jack Wilcox's death. By the time I do that, I'll have an idea."

"I hope so."

He rose from his chair. "Thanks for the coffee. And for telling me what you did."

Her eyes met his. "Oh, you didn't hear any of that from me."

"Of course."

Outside, having mounted up and hit the trail, he had plenty to think about. One thought that crossed his mind was that Claudette had known quite a bit. For her to have learned that much, and for Cliff Worthington to be as determined as he was to make her his, they must have gotten together in a familiar way more than once. Maybe she wanted to hang onto appearances with that one little lie, but overall, he thought she had come forth with decent intentions. As for the extent of her relations with Worthington, it was apparent that she wanted to stay away from the man. Alden was willing to leave it at that—put it in the past with the rest.

CHAPTER THIRTEEN

The sorrel horse was holding up well when Alden reached town. The sun had passed the midpoint in its daily course, and the main street lay quiet in the pale sunlight. Alden watched the street for a couple of minutes, then made a right turn and rode the short distance to the way station.

He found the Professor inside, reading a newspaper and chewing on a stick of licorice. At Alden's entrance, the Professor folded the newspaper and set it aside. He sat up straight in his chair and said, "You look as if you've been in a scrape. Did your horse throw you?"

"No. Cliff Worthington's men gave me a drubbing and took my horse and saddle."

"That's not good." The Professor leaned to one side and peered out the window. "What horse is that? One of Miller's?"

"Yes, but all of that's a lesser story, compared to the main reason I came here."

The Professor nodded. "Go ahead."

Alden spoke the words he had prepared earlier. "I came to report the death of Jack Wilcox. I was there when he died. According to his neighbor, Paul Sherwood, Cliff Worthington and his men started firing at them for no reason. When they rode up to the yard where I was talking with Bonnie Wilcox, Jack Wilcox had been shot and was still sitting in the saddle. Before he could get down from his horse, someone shot him in the back. I didn't get a good look, but I thought it was Cliff Worthington."

The Professor widened his eyes. "I agree that your own story is of lesser consequence, but none of this is good."

"I came to tell you so you could report it, to see if we can get someone from the law to come here."

"I should say so. I'll do it right away. Anything else?"

"I heard a story about Jack Wilcox's past life, but I suppose it can wait."

"Tell me quick. There might be something pertinent."

Alden had thought about how he would tell some of this story as well, so he launched in. "Well, the story as I heard it is that Jack Wilcox used to be a partner of Cliff Worthington's father. They robbed trains. On their last job, Worthington's father, whose name was not Worthington but something else I did not learn, was caught and sent to prison. Jack Wilcox, who was known as Black Jack Brody at the time, kept all the money for that job, while his partner died in prison. The son has carried the grudge, and that's why there's been so much trouble in and around the Hermit Flats."

The Professor gave a short, low whistle. "That's good information, if it's true. More than one party would be interested to know that Black Jack Brody might have been killed here. You know, the railroad has been looking for him for years—him, and the loot from the holdups." The Professor shifted in his chair. "I'd better get started sending this off. But before I do that, I want to ask you, do you go armed? This is dangerous stuff, even if you think you can take care of yourself."

"I've got my rifle along."

"That's good. I know you know how to use it. But let me give you a little help." The Professor opened the second drawer on the right side of his desk and drew out a shiny, blue-black revolver. As he handed it butt-first to Alden, he said, "This is a thirty-eight. It has great practical value. It's big enough for business and small enough to fit in your coat pocket. No one else needs to know you have it."

"Thanks," said Alden. "Does it have shells in it?"

"Five. Hammer's on an empty cylinder." The Professor reached into the drawer and brought out a small canvas bag with a braided cotton drawstring. "Here are some more cartridges. It loads pretty easy. Of course, I hope you don't have to use it."

"I might fire it once for practice, but I won't burn up all these shells on tin cans and jackrabbits." Alden put the pistol and the bag of cartridges in his right coat pocket.

"That's good. Now I'd better get busy sending this report. We can chat about other things later, or more about all of this."

"Good enough. I need to be going, too. Thanks for tending to this, and thanks for lending a helping hand. By the way, I didn't see Orval."

"He left."

"No trouble, I hope."

"No, he just left. I don't think he's the type to stay in one place for long. He finally saved enough so that he had a couple of coins to rub together, and he was gone. Honest fellow, as far as anything I saw. He just has the handicap of thinking people don't like him."

"Is he right?"

"Some of the time."

Alden raised his hand in a gesture of goodbye. "Very well. I'll be gone."

"Hie you to horse. Good luck, and be careful."

Alden kept a careful eye on his surroundings as he rode again toward the Hermit Flats. The sorrel horse did not radiate pep and energy, but it covered the ground at a steady pace. Alden longed to see Badger again, but he knew he had other things to tend to as well. In order to help Bonnie and Claudette both, he had to carry out his steps in a necessary order, which was going to be time-consuming.

He also knew that his plans could be upset at any time by an encounter with Worthington or his men. As he looked around him, he wished he had practiced firing the .38 while he was in town. Even a lone shot could draw attention out here. He patted his coat pocket and rode on, ever alert.

Nothing seemed to have changed as he rode up to the Wilcox homestead. Smoke from the stovepipe suggested that someone was at home. The two horses showed their heads over the corral rail.

Alden dismounted and called out. "Yoo-hoo! Anyone home?"

A minute later, Sooters appeared from around the corner of the house. He was wearing a winter cap and an oversized work coat, and his trouser cuffs piled up on his clodhopper shoes. He gave Alden a blank stare and stood silent.

Alden said, "I've come back from town. I reported what happened, and I'm here to help Bonnie with whatever she wants to do next."

Sooters blinked and said nothing.

"I hope it's all right if I go in and see her."

The kid shrugged and walked away, leaving Alden to assume he could follow.

Inside the house, he observed again the meager furnishings he had seen when they carried Jack in. The man lay on the floor in the front room with one grey blanket beneath him and another covering him from head to toe. His dusty black hat sat on top where his abdomen would be.

Bonnie stepped forward to meet Alden and gave him both hands. Her face was turbulent with grief, and her eyes were red and swollen. "I don't know what's to be done," she said.

Alden had to swallow before he could speak. "I reported the

shooting to Mr. Cameron Baker, the man I told you about who runs the telegraph office. The Professor. He said he would send it out right away, to see if we can't get some law here."

Bonnie nodded. She was not wearing her overcoat, and her dark hair was tied in braids. "I remember you saying his name before."

Paul Sherwood, who had been standing in the background, stepped forward. With greying stubble and his lips flapping on his loose mouth, he said, "A whole lot of good the law'll do when it gits here way late. We might all be dead by then. The high and mighty run over the little man like he was a field rat."

Alden looked at Bonnie. "I don't know if you want to take your father to town or keep him here."

"We can bury him here, on the place where he tried to make a living."

Sherwood said, "Costs money to bury someone in town, anyway."

"I know." Alden spoke again to Bonnie. "I want to help you, to the extent that I can, to protect what you've got here."

"Thank you. It's not much, but it's all we have."

He waited a few seconds to bring up his next point. "I have a request to make, and I hope you don't think it's out of order. If you do, that's all right."

Her eyes moved over him. "Go ahead."

"There's a girl I mentioned before, or perhaps I should say a woman. She was living with my brother, and she's on her own, even more so than you are, with no neighbors or anything. And she's got a little baby."

"I remember you mentioning her."

"So I feel kind of responsible for her, and I can't be in two places at once. What I was hoping to ask is whether I could bring her and her baby here for a couple of days. It wouldn't be for long. Then I would take them to town, and you could go, too, if you wanted. Depending on how you feel. For right now, I want to help both of you, and like I say, I can be in only one place at a time."

"Do you have a plan, then?"

"I think so. I can go to town, get a buggy, pick up Claudette and Florence, and be back here by about the middle of the day tomorrow."

"We have two horses and a wagon."

"It's good of you to offer. But I don't know how comfortable I would be with those two horses that I'm not familiar with."

Sherwood spoke again. "Just as well, Bonnie. Have somethin' happen to them horses, or the wagon, they're all you've got. And you don't know how the horses would act with someone else. You saw how that one threw me."

Alden recalled the incident, and he had the impression that Sherwood had lost either one stirrup or two and was bouncing around, and when the horse came jolting to a stop, Sherwood fell off.

Bonnie said, "Do what you think is best. If you want to bring her here for a day or two, that should be all right. We should hope these outlaws won't give trouble to women and children."

"I'll be here," said Alden. "That's the whole idea."

"Don't put it past 'em," said Sherwood. "They hazed me and your pa for a long time with no good reason, and they opened up on us this morning, again with no reason. Just pure bad nature."

From the time Claudette had told Alden the story of Black Jack Brody, he was sure he would have to be the one to tell Bonnie. But with her father lying on the floor in the same room, having died earlier that day, Alden did not think this was any time to tell what he knew.

He said, "Maybe it's hard to know how much of the whole story there is."

Sherwood smacked his lips and said, "What else is there?"

Alden shrugged. "Maybe time will tell."

Mounted on the sorrel horse with his rifle and scabbard beneath his leg, Alden again avoided the spot where Blodgett and Oates had beat him up. He needed to make good time in order to arrive in town before dark, so he made but a minimal detour. He had a sense of the breaks lying a few miles away to the southeast. From time to time he scanned the country in that direction, to his right, but nothing appeared except the normal rises and dips of rolling grassland dotted with sage.

A cold breeze was picking up from the northwest, so he tipped his head and hunched his shoulder on the left. The low shadows on the rangeland began to lengthen. Calculating that he had more than half the distance to cover, he gigged the sorrel horse with his spurs.

A band of about fifteen antelope came running up over a rise on the trail ahead. Seeing him, they veered to their right and kept running.

He stopped for a moment, letting the animals go on their way. He reflected that it was normal to see antelope in groups that size and bigger at this time of year. He watched them as they streaked to the west, strung out in a line. Then, remembering that time was pressing, he spurred the sorrel again.

Within a couple of minutes, the horse brought him to the low crest that the antelope had passed over. As he scanned the country ahead of him on the other side, he felt a thump in the pit of his stomach. A quarter of a mile ahead, Blodgett and Oates were riding his way. Blodgett was on Alden's left, riding a dark horse, while on his right, Oates was riding Badger.

Alden's heart was pounding. When the two oncoming riders kicked their horses into a lope, he turned the sorrel around and headed back over the hill. The sorrel loped, but not very fast, as he had put in quite a few miles that day and was not a fleet-footed animal to begin with. Alden was sure that Blodgett and Oates could catch him, and he didn't want them to come up on him from behind. They could shoot him, rope him, or, like the day before, haze him close and pull him off his horse. When he reached a flat, open spot, he brought the sorrel to a stop, dismounted, and turned the horse to serve as a barrier between him and the other two riders.

He pulled the rifle from the scabbard, levered in a shell, and got ready.

Blodgett and Oates came up over the rise on a run. At sight of him, they slowed to a stop, then separated and rode toward him at a fast walk. Two hundred yards away, they broke into a gallop. They had their pistols drawn and began shooting. Bullets dug up spurts of dust from the ground nearby.

Alden clenched his teeth. He was not going to let them do what they had done before—or worse. Using the sorrel horse for cover, he raised his rifle into shooting position. Then he stepped forward, pulled the sorrel horse aside, drew a bead on George Oates, and fired.

Oates lurched, leaned forward, and clasped his right hand to his ribs. He bobbled in the saddle and fell off, while Badger kept running.

Alden kept his eyes on Blodgett. The man in the black hat and sheepskin coat stopped his horse and reined it so that its head and neck blocked out most of the rider's upper body. Alden followed the man's gaze.

George Oates was sitting on the prairie, bare-headed, clutch-ing his midsection with both hands. At a hundred yards away, he made an easy target, but his pleading voice made him seem too personal for Alden to fire again.

"Art! Come and get me. I'm hurt bad."

Alden focused on Blodgett again. So far, this was rifle range, not pistol. If Blodgett stepped down and pulled a rifle, Alden was going to have to shoot, even if it meant hitting a horse.

Oates called again. "Art! I'm hurt bad."

Blodgett spurred his horse and cut toward Oates, raising his pistol and firing in Alden's direction as he did so. Alden stepped back and fought the reins of the sorrel horse, trying to keep the animal for cover, as bullets kicked up dirt around him.

Blodgett had his back to Alden for a second, then whirled the horse and reached down toward his partner on the other side. Within a few seconds, Oates, in his grey wool overcoat, climbed up onto the back of Blodgett's horse like a big barnyard cat. He hung onto the man in the sheepskin coat, who leaned forward and spurred the horse into a gallop.

Alden raised his rifle, but he did not have a shot at a clear target, and he did not want to shoot at the mass. He watched as the horse and two riders moved away—not in the direction from which they had come, but south toward the breaks.

Alden turned his attention now toward Badger. He searched for a full hundred-and-eighty degrees until he saw the horse a quarter of a mile away. His heart lifted at the sight of his grey horse with dark ears, mane, and tail. Badger.

Casting an eye again toward the south, Alden stowed the rifle in the scabbard. The sorrel was a bit jumpy, not its usual placid self, which was no surprise after all the gunfire. Even though Alden knew it was easier to catch another horse by riding up to it, he decided to lead the sorrel and approach Badger on foot.

As he feared, Badger was skittish as well. Each time Alden came within a hundred yards, Badger would trot away another hundred. Alden called his name and spoke to him, and Badger would look over his shoulder with no alarm, but he kept his distance. After three or four exercises at stop-and-go, Alden held the sorrel horse still and climbed aboard. The sorrel was calm again, and this time, Badger allowed Alden to ride alongside and lay a hand on his reins. Alden felt a rush of relief, a wave of happiness. His horse had someone else's saddle and blanket, but this was his horse, in his hands again. Badger.

In town, Alden made arrangements to spend the night in the livery stable. He did not tell Joe any details about how he came to have two saddled horses, and he thought the stable man regarded them with interest. If Joe noticed that neither saddle was Alden's, or that one had blood on it, he did not let on.

At a distance he had paced off at fifty feet, Alden raised the pistol, cocked it, and lined up the sights on the empty whiskey bottle. The clear glass reflected the morning sunlight, as did several other bottles in the rubbish heap. After riding for miles and miles in open country where he should not have been a bother to anyone, he had to resort to shooting at a whiskey bottle on the edge of town. He planned to shoot only once or twice, and no one would pay him much mind.

Alden held the .38 as steady as he could with one hand. When the front sight settled into the notch, he waited a second or two until the target, the sights, his breath, and his heartbeat all came together. He pulled the trigger, and the tip of the barrel lifted as the blast shattered the stillness of the morning. The bottle exploded into flying fragments and slivers.

A voice from behind made his pulse jump. "Not bad." It was a man's voice, but the utterance was not long enough for Alden to recognize the speaker. Relaxing his arm and lowering the pistol partway, he turned to see a man wearing a capote made of coyote furs. Alden had positioned himself to shoot with the sun at his back, and now he had it in his eyes. He squinted as he tried to identify the bearded face inside the fur hood.

"Bill Smith," said the onlooker. "From Shawnee."

"Oh, yes. The hunter."

Bill shrugged. "Sometimes. You're doin' all the shootin' at the moment."

"Not much. And I'm not hunting."

"Maybe not. But if you're a hunter, you hunt every day in one way or another, even when you've got no gun at all."

"I guess you're right." Alden held the revolver at his side. He kept in mind the Professor's suggestion that no one needed to know he had it in his pocket, and even though he trusted Bill Smith, he was in no hurry to show him where he kept his pistol. He tipped his head and said, "What brings you here today?"

He walked toward Bill, motioned with his hat brim toward town, and fell into an easy stroll. As Bill turned and kept him company on the left side, Alden slipped the gun into his right coat pocket. He wondered if Bill paid any attention.

"Sorry to hear about your brother."

"It was hard to take. Thanks for the thought."

"Sometimes it don't seem fair. But you can't change it."

"I've come to see that."

Bill walked along for several steps until he spoke again. "Wonder about that girl he was with."

Ah, thought Alden. "A lot has happened since you were here," he said. "Another fellow has been hanging around, but nothing seems to be taking shape there."

"But she's not with anyone right now, then?"

"Just her little one. She's got a baby."

"Huh. I don't think I knew that."

"Just one. Actually, she had it the last time you asked about her, but I don't believe it got mentioned."

Bill seemed to give the matter a moment's assessment. "Well," he said, "it could be worse." After another pause, he asked, "She still live in the same place?"

"Yes, she does. As far as that goes, I'm planning to go there in a little while. You could ride along if you'd like."

"Might could. When do you think you'll go?"

"As soon as I can get a buggy ready."

"Oh."

"Don't worry about me. I've got my eye on another girl, quite a bit different from her."

"That's good to know." After a few seconds, Bill said, "Be ready in a little while, huh?"

"Yep."

"I'll ride along, then, since you invited me."

"Good. I could use the company."

They walked for another minute until Bill spoke.

"By the way, I know where you can get a holster for that thirty-eight if you need one."

Having left Miller's sorrel at the livery stable, and having left George Oates's saddle with the Professor along with a brief account of the run-in, Alden drove the carriage along the familiar trail toward the bungalow. Badger trotted along behind, tied by a halter and rope and fitted out with Miller's saddle.

Bill Smith rode alongside. As the sun rose in the sky and took some of the chill out of the air, Bill set back the hood of his fur overcoat and put on a brown wool winter cap with a short beak. His eyes kept watch over the rangeland, and as usual, he did not speak much.

Alden brought the buggy to a stop outside the bungalow, and the door opened. He figured Claudette must have seen them coming, for she was wearing not only her attractive blue sweater but what looked like a fresh application of lipstick.

As she stepped out onto the doorstep, Alden spoke across the short distance. "How-de-do? You remember Bill Smith, from Shawnee, don't you?" Alden turned and nodded toward Bill, who had dismounted.

Her eyes had a shine as she turned them toward Bill. "Of

course I do. It's good to meet you again. My name's Claudette."

Bill took off his cap and held it at chest level. "The pleasure's all mine," he said.

Silence hung in the air until Alden spoke. "Bill came along to lend a hand and keep us company. By the way, I've arranged for us to go to Bonnie Wilcox's place first, and after a short stay there, we can go on to town."

"Why can't we just go to town now?"

Alden had to push himself to be firm. "I need to help her through this hard time, and I'd told you I'd help you get away from here as soon as I could, and this is the only way I can do both. You weren't planning to take everything today anyway, were you?"

The sparkle was gone from her eyes as they met his. "Well, no."

"Everything should be all right, then, especially if we all hang together." He considered whether to tell her about his most recent run-in with Blodgett and Oates, and he decided he would tell her later. To keep things simple, he said, "I've given Bill something of a background on the whole situation."

Her eyes took on some life again as she turned her attention toward Bill. "I hope you don't think I'm bad luck."

Alden realized that Claudette's idea of background pertained to her own situation, while he had meant his own conflict and the troubles at the Hermit Flats as well.

Bill smiled in response as his eyes held on her. "I'm not very superstitious," he said.

CHAPTER FOURTEEN

Paul Sherwood and Sooters stood back as Alden introduced Claudette and Bill Smith to Bonnie. The group of six people stood on the east side of the house, out of the chilly breeze that blew from the west. Pale sunlight showed from overhead, but Alden felt a bleakness about the scene, as if they had gathered outside the church after a funeral.

"Don't mind me," said Sherwood. "I'm just the neighbor. This is my boy, Sooters. We been helpin' out." He lifted a cigarette to his lips. "We buried Jack this mornin'."

Claudette touched Bonnie's arm and said, "I'm very sorry for what happened to your father."

"Thank, you," said Bonnie. "I understand you've had your troubles, too. I hope we all get through it all right."

Alden observed the scene for a moment—one dark-haired girl and one light-haired girl, quite different in their life experiences but both young women who, early in life's journey, had been made to suffer because of men's violence to one another. Jack Wilcox's death, being more recent and having occurred in this place, had more presence, but as Alden had sifted things out, Jack may well have brought about the death of little Florence's father.

Sherwood spoke up again. "They been watchin' us with field glasses."

"Where from?" Alden asked.

Sherwood pointed with his thumb. "From those hills over on

the north. That's the closest you can get without bein' seen. But the sun shines off their glasses."

Alden said, "The best thing is not to provoke them." He glanced at Bill Smith. "Shall we put things away?"

Bill seemed glad to have something to do. "Might as well," he said. Then to Claudette, "I'll bring in that bundle of blankets and baby stuff."

She turned her eyes to him. "Thank you."

"This way," said Bonnie.

Paul Sherwood stood by, smoking another cigarette in the company of his sullen understudy, as Bill moved items into the house and Alden unhitched the buggy horse.

"Wal," said Sherwood, "I think you can find your way around. Me 'n' Sooters can go on home and take care of things there. C'mon, boy."

"So long," said Alden.

"Let me know if you need anything." Sherwood ambled away, cigarette smoke trailing on the breeze. Sooters walked alongside in his baggy coat and pants.

As Alden put the rented horse and Badger in the corral, he studied the layout. Although he had visited the homestead several times, he hadn't seen much. Now he had a fuller view.

The house faced east. Around the corner to the left, the building faced south, where the ranch wagon was parked and where Sooters had skinned an antelope one cold day almost a year earlier. Southwest of the house, almost touching it corner to corner, the corrals began. The two Wilcox horses stood in the nearest pen, then a cow and a calf, and then the corral where Alden turned Badger in with the buggy horse. West of the corrals sat a small mound of firewood, a manure pile, and a rubbish heap. Straight west of the house a few yards stood a shed about twelve feet wide and twenty-four feet long. Alden peeked in and saw what he expected—saddles and harness hanging on one wall, long-handled tools leaning together in one corner, a heap of gunny sacks, a grain box, and a wheelbarrow.

Outside, Alden met up with Bill Smith, who had brought his horse around from in front of the house.

Alden said, "I think we can put our gear in this shed, and you can turn your horse in with mine."

"Good enough."

"And I think we can make enough room for our bedrolls as well."

"Sleep in the shed?"

"That's what I thought. I don't know if it would be proper for us to sleep under the same roof with those girls."

Bill drew his mouth together and raised his eyebrows. "It wouldn't bother me so much, but whatever you think is best."

"You never know what someone like this neighbor is going to say."

"He does flap his jaws a little."

Bill Smith pitched hay as Alden pumped and carried water for all the livestock. Sundown came early and fast, as it did in November, and the night grew cold. Bill put away the pitchfork and slapped his large, gloved hands together. "I can smell the grub cookin' from out here. Seems to me we missed a meal at noontime."

"I noticed that, too," said Alden. "Let's go in and see what's for supper."

Inside, the combination of light, warmth, and the aroma of fried food picked up Alden's spirits. Claudette had brought along the remainder of antelope meat, and she and Bonnie had fried it in bacon grease. In a second skillet, thick slices of potato glistened brown and golden.

"Here," said Claudette to Bonnie. "Why don't you have a seat? There's not much room to move in, and it only takes one of us to serve up the food. If you hand me the plates, I'll do them one by one."

Alden took a seat across from Bonnie. Having taken off his hat and washed his hands, he felt quite dutiful. He stole a glance at Bill Smith, who kept his eye on Claudette. Alden thought she was taking the opportunity to shine in the kitchen and was doing well at it. He reflected on the old saying that the way to a man's heart was through his stomach. He thought Claudette had already done plenty, without trying, to win over Bill Smith. Now as she made her smooth movements in her snug apron, it was as if she was suggesting the promise of apple pie after the meat and potatoes.

Bill Smith was hanging the lantern on a nail in the shed, and Alden was deciding how he wanted to roll out his blankets, when hoofbeats sounded. A man's voice carried, but Alden could not make out the words.

Bill said, "I think we best put out this light."

"Let me pull out my rifle first."

"Wouldn't you know it? The one time I didn't bring a rifle."

"I'm sure there's one in the house." An image of the defiant Jack Wilcox passed through Alden's mind. He bent over his saddle and slid the rifle from its scabbard. "I've got it," he said. "You can blow out the light if you want."

Outside, Alden saw light flickering past the front of the house. He and Bill headed for the back door, from which they had left the house a few minutes earlier. Bill went up the steps first.

"Locked," he said.

"The girls are probably in front. We'd have to holler to tell 'em to open up. How about one of us goes around each side?"

"I 'magine." Bill drew his pistol and set off around the south side of the house, leaving Alden to go along the north.

Rays of light danced and hoofbeats sounded, as if a couple of riders were pacing back and forth. As Alden paused at the front corner of the house, he heard Worthington's voice loud and commanding.

"Claudette, you come out, and we'll leave everyone else alone. But you come out."

A woman's voice sounded from within the house. "Go away!" Alden thought she might be hollering through a closed door.

"I said come out! If you don't, we'll burn this place to the ground."

Now Bonnie's voice sounded, clearer, as if she had opened the door. "Go away. You've already got enough blood on your hands."

Worthington's voice rose in a sneer. "Is that you, Missy? Black Jack's daughter. Well, let me tell you what. Be best for you to stay out of this. Your father was a no-good, double-crossin' son of a bitch that finally got what he deserved. But when I get even, I get even. There's nothin' tells me I have to quit now. So just shut your trap, Miss Puss, and tell Claudette to come out."

Alden had edged up to the corner, ever so slow in his movements, as Worthington made his speech, and now Alden had a view. Two riders, each carrying a torch, were visible in the flickering light. Blodgett's dark horse was pacing a couple of steps to each side. Worthington's horse had come to a stop, and Alden had the man in his rifle sights. He was tempted to pull the trigger for the way Worthington had talked to Bonnie, but he had to restrain himself. Shooting like this could be seen as an ambush, in cold blood, and he could be found guilty of it. Moreover, it did not seem right. He would have to wait until the outlaws made a move. He imagined Bill Smith was thinking in a similar way.

Claudette's voice came out clear on the night air. "Go away. You've caused more than enough grief for everyone."

Worthington raised his head in the torchlight and said, "Come out of there. You're going to be mine. I tell you, I get what I want, so you can make it easy on everyone. Just—"

Her voice cut him short. "Go to hell."

Even at a distance of fifty feet in imperfect light, the resentment on Worthington's face was visible. "Well, piss on the whole bunch of you!" he called out. He spurred his horse forward, turned it in a half-circle in front of the house, and tossed his torch up onto the roof. He kept his horse in a circle and came around again with his six-shooter drawn. He fired one shot after another into the front of the house, breaking a window and causing the women inside to shriek.

Alden was trying to draw a bead, but Worthington was moving in and out of the light and was then blocked from view as Blodgett came riding forward. Like his boss, he tossed his torch onto the roof of the house, circled around, and began shooting.

Alden lined up on the sheepskin coat and pulled the trigger. He heard the shot go home as Blodgett rose in the saddle.

The man hunched over, making a belly-deep sound like a wounded buck. *"Aah-rugh!"* He showed amazing control as he holstered his pistol, hung onto his reins, and grabbed the saddle horn with both hands. He rocked back and forth as he galloped away into the night.

Quiet held for a moment until Bill Smith called out. "Girls! Open up the back door for us. The roof's on fire. Get your things together."

From somewhere beyond the firelight, a series of four pistol shots sounded, and bullets pelted the house like hail.

Alden fired a rifle shot in the direction he thought the shots came from, and then he held back. He did not want to seem like a fool by firing wide and wasting ammunition.

No more shots came. Alden made his way to the back door, where he met with Bill Smith. Half a minute later, the door opened, and Bonnie handed them the two tin buckets they had used for bringing in water to wash the dishes and clean up after supper.

"Here," she said. "We're getting together what blankets and clothes we can. Shall we put them in the wagon or in the shed?"

"In the shed," said Alden. "I don't think we want to try going anywhere in the dark."

Bill took the buckets. "I'll fill these," he said.

Alden took Bonnie's hands in his. "I'm sorry for this," he said.

"No reason to be," she answered. "From what he said, I imagine he would have wanted to set fire to us sooner or later anyway." Claudette's voice sounded from within, and Bonnie called over her shoulder, "I'm coming."

Alden hurried to the pump, where Bill was filling the second bucket.

Bill said, "If you can boost me to the roof and hand me these two, I'll try to put the fire out." He picked up the two buckets and took off on a low run.

Alden caught up with him and set his rifle against the house. "It's a ways up," he said.

"Not too bad."

Alden held his hands together to make a step. Bill put his left boot in the makeshift stirrup, pressed his left hand down on the top of Alden's hat, and reached up with his right hand as Alden lifted and pushed. Bill's feet dangled as he hoisted himself and squirmed up onto the roof.

Bill turned around, kneeling, and reached down as Alden raised the two buckets, pushing the bottom of each one with his fingertips. Footsteps sounded on the dry wood shingles as Bill hustled forward with the water.

Alden stood back and watched the silhouette as Bill pitched the contents of the two buckets.

A rifle shot rang out, followed by another as Bill came scurrying back.

"The fire's caught pretty good hold already. I don't know if we could get water up here fast enough even if someone wasn't shooting at us."

"How about wet blankets or gunny sacks?"

"It's burning through the roof in one spot already. So it's not all on the surface."

"Oh. Well, let's try two more."

"Go ahead."

Bonnie came out of the house with an armload of blankets. Claudette was a few steps behind, clutching a smaller bundle of blankets along with the crying baby.

"The house is filling up with smoke," she said.

"Bill said the fire is through the roof. Things could start falling in pretty soon. Be careful about going back in. I've got to fill these buckets."

He ran to the pump, worked the handle as fast as he could, and hurried back to the house in a low run as Bill had done.

"It's goin' fast," said Bill as he reached for the first bucket. "I'll throw these on, just because we have 'em."

Another shot rang out as Bill pitched the water. He came scooting back along the roof and tossed the pails one by one to Alden.

"I think it's a lost cause," he said. "I'm comin' down."

"Do you need help?"

"Not yet." He bailed off, landing on his feet with a thump.

Bonnie returned from the shed and came to a stop, breathing hard. "I don't know if I should go back in."

Bill said, "Does your pa have a rifle?"

"It's in the front room, over on the left side."

Bill shook his head. "That part's fallin' in already. If there's anything in the back part of the house, we can try to save it."

"Maybe some clothes. We don't have much anyway."

"I'll go with you," said Alden.

Bill said, "I'll keep a lookout at the shed. You don't know what they'll try next."

Alden took Bonnie's hand and led the way up the steps to the back door. When he pushed it open, he was met with a rush of heat and smoke.

"I don't know," he said. "It doesn't look good."

At that moment, part of the roof in the front part of the house fell in, causing a shower of sparks and flame some fifteen feet away.

"Let it go," said Bonnie. She was standing on the step below him, and the fire lit up the lost expression on her face.

Back on solid ground, Alden looked around until he found his rifle where he had set it against the house. "Let's go to the shed," he said.

The burning house was casting light a long ways out. Bill was standing in shadow on the south side of the shed. Alden joined him as Bonnie went inside.

"Pity to lose that rifle," Bill said. "At least you've got yours."

"I'm hoping we're down to just one man against us."

"I think you hit the other one pretty good."

"Small comfort," said Alden. "I wish this last one would take his losses and pull out, but he doesn't seem to think that way."

"Whatever he thinks, it's not good."

No more gunshots came out of the night, and within an hour, the wood frame house had burned to the ground. The firelight died down, but the smell of burnt cloth and scorched cotton stuffing hung in the air. In the glow of embers, some objects were identifiable—a washtub, a kerosene can, a couple of metal bed frames, and the cookstove with a skillet still on top.

By midnight, most of the glow had died away, though smoky odors still drifted on the cold air. Bill and Alden agreed to take two-hour shifts on guard outside. Bill took the first shift, and Alden covered up a few feet away from Bonnie, Claudette, and the baby.

Alden had barely fallen asleep, it seemed, when Bill shook him and spoke in a low voice.

"Your turn, partner."

Alden gave his bed to Bill and crept outside to stand, or rather sit, at guard against the door of the shed. He covered up with the horse blankets that Bill had used, and with the rifle in his lap, he gazed at the faint embers. His eyelids grew heavy, and he fought to stay awake.

A cold object against his nose woke him. The night was still dark. No light of predawn was showing yet. The cold thing pushed, and he moved his head away from it. The cold thing followed.

A low voice said, "Don't make a sound, sonny boy."

Alden had his eyes wide open. The cold object was a pistol barrel, and crouched at his left side was Cliff Worthington. The man wore a close-fitting winter cap, and his birdlike nose was visible in the starlight. Worthington held his pistol with one hand. With the other, he held Alden's rifle upright, like a staff, to steady himself as he crouched.

Worthington spoke in a whisper. "Stand up real slow so we can open the door. One wrong move, and this gun goes off."

Alden pushed the horse blankets aside, put his hands beneath him, and pushed himself upward from the cold ground. His gloves were in his left coat pocket. He had slept with his hands beneath his crossed arms so that he could handle the rifle or the .38 if he had to. Now Worthington had the rifle.

As they came to their feet together, Worthington kept the tip of the barrel pushed against Alden's face. As they both turned to face the door, Worthington stepped around to stay on Alden's left side.

Alden's right hand found his coat pocket and settled on the pistol. He put his thumb on the hammer and his finger near the trigger. With his left hand, he opened the door and stepped back.

Worthington spoke, just a little louder than a whisper. "Light a match."

"I don't have one."

Worthington's nose whistled as he took in an impatient breath. "Just a second." With his handgun still pointed at Alden, he leaned the rifle against the open door.

Alden came around with the .38 and shot him point blank in the chest. The muzzle blast set out a glow of light, showing Worthington's pale mustache, birdlike nose, and surprised eyes.

The women screamed, baby Florence cried out, and Bill Smith sprang up in the darkness. His pistol clicked as he said, "What the hell?"

"I got him," said Alden. "He took me by surprise, but I got him." His heart was pounding, and his hand was shaking. He did not want to say any more because he thought his voice would quaver.

Bill lit the lantern. Claudette and Bonnie were both sitting up, fully clothed, with blankets draped around them. Claudette held the baby close and patted her.

After a few breaths, Alden spoke. "It's my fault. I couldn't stay awake. He came up on me and got the drop on me."

"It's all right now," said Bill as he held the lantern over the body.

At daybreak, Alden built a fire outside, using firewood from the woodpile. After the conflagration the night before, the campfire seemed minuscule, but it began to seem normal as the others gathered around. Nobody had slept any more but had huddled in blankets in the shed, waiting for the dawn. Bonnie and Claudette still had blankets wrapped around them as they sat by the fire.

Bill Smith, standing near, motioned with a large gloved hand in the direction where he and Alden had dragged Worthington's body out of view. "At least there's an end to him," he said.

Bonnie stared at the fire. "After all the trouble he caused."

Claudette gathered her blanket around Florence. "He didn't know when to quit."

Bonnie frowned. "One thing I don't understand. Why he said what he did about my father."

Alden glanced at Claudette, who relaxed her eyes and looked away. *It's up to me,* he thought. He laid a piece of wood on the fire and stood up. "I heard a little bit, not long ago." He met Bonnie's eyes. "I'm sorry to have to tell it."

She blinked and said, "Go ahead."

"Well, the way I heard it, Jack was partners with Worthington's father. They robbed trains. Jack was known as Black Jack Brody. On their last job, the partner got caught and sent off to jail. Jack made away with all the money, but he didn't hang onto it. He squandered it. Then he showed up here, after living for a great many years, I guess, as Jack Wilcox."

Bonnie nodded. "And the partner?"

"He died in prison. He never turned witness against Jack, but he never forgave him. Neither did his son, of course. We've seen plenty of evidence of that."

"And the partner's name?"

"It wasn't Worthington, from what I heard. His first name was Frank, but I don't know what his real last name was."

"Trimble," said Claudette. She did not look up from the fire. "Frank Trimble. The convicted train robber." She tossed a glance in the direction of the body. "You can change your name, but you can't change the truth. And when you're dead, it's all the same." She softened her eyes and turned to Bonnie. "I'm sorry. Maybe that's a little strong. I wasn't thinking of you when I said it."

Bonnie gave a mild shake of the head. "It's all right. I just have to accept it."

Bill Smith rode with Alden to the breaks, where they found the camp. Oates and Blodgett lay side by side, stone cold dead. Not far away, Alden found his saddle.

"I'm glad to get this back," he said.

"Good for you," said Bill. He had his hood laid back and was wearing his brown cap. He motioned with his chin. "Hate to see a good sheepskin coat go to waste, but I suppose that's one of the smaller details."

Alden shook his head. "So much waste of life and everything else. And none of it had to happen."

Bill shrugged. "Their choice."

CHAPTER FIFTEEN

The bell made a ringing, tinkling sound as Alden opened the door and walked into Julia Redwine's dry goods store. Straightway down the center aisle, Bonnie appeared in front of the sales counter. She was wearing a sky-blue dress, and she had her dark hair tied back behind her shoulders. She walked forward to meet him. Holding her hands together in front of her waist, she said, "Good evening. You might be a few minutes early, but that's fine. Mr. Baker is already here."

Alden took off his hat and smiled as he held it by his side.

"I'll close the door," she said, "even if it's not quite the hour." She walked past him and turned the latch on the door.

As she approached him again, he said, "That's a nice-looking dress."

"Thank you. I think I mentioned that Julia has been letting me use her sewing machine."

"Yes, you did." He wanted to touch the soft wool fabric as she stood in front of him. "And you made this dress yourself?"

Bonnie smiled, almost bashful. "Julia helped me a little, but I'm learning a great deal."

He turned and made a waving motion with his hat in the direction of the shelves of fabric, thread, needles, and other notions. "You're certainly in a good place for it."

Her eyes sparkled as she smiled again. "Isn't it, though?"

He reached for her hand, and she gave it to him. "I'm so glad you're doing well here," he said.

"Julia has been very easy to get along with. She has plenty of work for me, to be sure, on into the evening with the children, but she's never cross, and she leaves me a little time for myself."

"To sew?"

"And read. She has a few books." Bonnie released his hand. "Let's go ahead."

She led the way to the back of the store and into the kitchen area. Alden recalled having been in that part of the building once, the evening he carried in the deer meat and met Jack and Bonnie on the way out. The area was brighter now, lit with two lamps.

The Professor stood by the stove in something of a domestic pose, wearing a white apron and holding a carving knife and fork in his hands. Beneath the apron, he wore a brown jacket and vest, a white shirt, and a black tie.

His glasses raised as he scrunched his nose. "Glad you made it," he said. "This chicken is cooked perfect, and I wouldn't want you to miss out."

Julia stepped around him, opened the oven door, and took out a golden-brown roasted fowl. The aroma wafted on the warm air rising out of the oven.

"This is the last of Claudette's chickens," she said as she set the metal tray on the sideboard. She stepped aside and smoothed her apron, white against the tan background of her dress.

Alden directed a calm glance at the Professor. "Did you do the deed?"

"Take its life? I'm afraid I did. Miss Bonnie offered to, but I spared her the trouble. She works hard enough, milking the cow."

"She's a dear," said Julia. "She helps me so much."

Alden's eyes met Bonnie's, and she gave a modest smile.

Julia held the tray as the Professor began to carve. "I heard from Claudette just a couple of days ago. A short letter. She doesn't write long ones. But she seems to be doing well with Mr. Smith in Shawnee."

"She's now Mrs. Smith," the Professor added. "He seems like a good, sturdy fellow."

"I believe he is," said Alden.

"Here's the first cut. Ah, cooked just right, my dear."

Alden was startled at the Professor's cozy manner of address, until he realized that the Professor was speaking to the chicken and not to Julia.

"You were such a plump little thing the day you met the knife."

Julia stood back and smoothed her dark hair. She seemed to be accustomed to the Professor's quaint way of speaking. "Won't the two of you sit down? The children already ate, by the way."

Alden and Bonnie sat down, and within a few minutes, Julia and the Professor took their seats. As the meal got under way, the conversation came around to a more serious topic than the fate of the chicken. Representatives of the railroad had come to town, and the Professor had caught the drift of their purposes.

"They've got no mercy," he said. "Everyone who deals with them learns that, sooner or later. Even people who have a good case rarely win."

Julia passed around a basket of bread.

The Professor continued. "In the matter of young Worthington, or Trimble, as it turns out, there's not anyone to contest the claim, even if there were justification. Which there doesn't seem to be. The railroad has a good case that the ranch over there south of Silver Springs was bought with the long-hoarded proceeds of the train holdups. The railroad files a claim or a lien against the property, and good luck to anyone who might want to fight it."

Alden caught a glance from Bonnie, and he thought he

understood it. Directing his words to the Professor, he said, "And is something similar under way out in the area of the Hermit Flats?"

"There seems to be. And I don't mean to be speaking for you, Miss Bonnie."

"Please go ahead. I'd rather you than me. Or I."

"Correct." The Professor took a piece of bread and set the basket to the side. "It's all rather disheartening, but as I said, the railroad is relentless. Even in the case of something of small value, they want to win."

Alden met Bonnie's eyes again. "I'm sorry to hear that," he said.

"It's all right," she answered in a steady voice. "I don't know that I would want something that came from what you would call ill gains. But he was my father, and that means something."

Julia put her hand on Bonnie's. "Of course it does, dear."

Alden blinked and hoped he did not have to wipe away a tear. He gave a small cough to clear the thickness in his throat. "I'd be glad to go out there with you if you'd like, before they get their hands on it."

"I would like that," she said. "But let's not be too sad this evening. I don't want to spoil this nice occasion."

Alden looked around as if he had missed something.

"Just a sociable dinner among friends," said the Professor. "And our hostess may have an eponymous beverage for us."

"Eponymous?" said Alden.

"Named for her."

"I have a bottle of red wine," said Julia. "No special occasion. As Mr. Baker said, just a pleasant evening among friends."

With the days growing longer and the sun a little warmer, Alden and Bonnie rode on horseback to the Hermit Flats—he on Badger, and she on the stout sorrel. A dry breeze blew from the southwest as they stood by the ruins of the house.

"I'm sorry to see you lose this," he said.

"It's not much, and I suppose that in some way it's not mine."

"Still, to be left without anything. I know how it feels, because I went through the same thing with my own family's property. I'm sure I'll never get it back at this point. The last I heard, the bank was consolidating it with a couple of other foreclosed properties, including the place where Claudette lived, and selling it all together."

"It's not as if I didn't get anything," she said. "As you know, I was able to salvage and sell the horses, the wagon, and the few head of cattle we had. That money's safe, and with me working for Julia, I don't have to ask anyone for anything." She handed him the reins and made a tight smile. "If you could hold this, I'd like to go visit with my papa."

He felt a burning in his nose, and he made an effort to hold back any moisture in his eyes. "Sure," he said.

He did not watch her but left her to be alone with her father. He gazed at the surrounding country, spare as always, and brought his eyes to rest again on the charred remains of the house. The black spot seemed like a scar on the landscape, and he wondered how much the blight of Black Jack Wilcox, or Brody, would weigh on the future. Not too much, he hoped, yet he knew the past would not vanish for good.

Light footsteps sounded, and then her voice. "I think we can go now."

As they rode toward town in the faint warmth of early spring, he said, "Let's go by way of Castle Butte. It's a pleasure to see at this time of year, when the country is beginning to green up again."

She sniffled and said, "That way's fine with me."

"I'm sorry," he said. "Maybe at the moment there doesn't seem much to be happy about."

She heaved out a short breath. "It's all right. I'm trying to make my way through these bad circumstances and put them in the past."

They rode for several minutes until he spoke again. "I need to be looking ahead, too. Miller will be coming back before long, middle of April, and I'll need to make a move. I can go back to work for Willis Squire and put together a little more money." After the horses moved on a few more paces, he said, "We could make a go of it if we were both on foot and in rags, but I'd rather not go into things without a nickel. I know we've talked about this, but I don't mind saying it again. There's no need to be in a hurry."

She gave a short, nervous-like laugh. "Oh, no. And it's not just the money. Florence was a lovely little thing, and Julia's children are sweet as well, but as you and I have also agreed, there's no need to be in a hurry about that part, either." She rode close and took his hand. "We're not that old yet."

He leaned over and kissed her. "I know."

She straightened up, and in a clear voice she said, "I've decided to buy a sewing machine. With the money I made from selling our things, the horses and all, I can buy a new one."

He was impressed by her resolve. "You like sewing, then."

"I like making things that are pleasing as well as useful."

As he met her dark eyes, he took the courage to say, "I imagine you'll want a place for your sewing machine."

Her eyes took on a shine. "And I imagine you'll want a place for your bookcase."

"Oh, yes. And you say you've been reading?" Upon reflection, he realized that her manner of speaking had risen perhaps a notch since he first met her.

"Yes," she said. "I just finished *Uncle Tom's Cabin*."

"That's good."

"Mrs. Stowe was a brave woman for writing that book."

"I suppose she was."

"President Lincoln said so."

"I didn't know that." Alden gave Bonnie a close look. "I have the feeling that you might like to write something yourself someday."

"I don't know. I might. But first I'd have to read a great deal more."

"All the more reason to have a place for a bookcase. You know, in spite of the difficulties, I still believe in the value of having one's own land."

"So do I."

He rode closer so that his leg touched hers. This time he took her in his arms and kissed her, and the horses stopped.

"I've been wanting to tell you for a long time that I love you, Bonnie. I guess I should have said it sooner. We've already talked about everything else."

"I didn't mind waiting, but I'm glad you said it. I love you, too, Alden."

He settled back into his saddle, and the horses moved on. He thought he might get things in the right order yet. "Well, how about that bookcase and sewing machine?"

"It sounds fine."

"And a place to put them."

"That, too."

"I have to admit there's another reason I wanted to go this way today."

"What's that?"

"There's a place I wanted to show you. Not very big, just a hundred-and-sixty acres, but a piece of land for sale on the other side of Castle Butte."

ABOUT THE AUTHOR

John D. Nesbitt lives in the plains country of Wyoming, where he teaches English and Spanish at Eastern Wyoming College. He writes western, contemporary, mystery, and retro/noir fiction as well as nonfiction and poetry. John has won many awards for his work, including two awards from the Wyoming State Historical Society (for fiction), two awards from Wyoming Writers for encouragement of other writers and service to the organization, two Wyoming Arts Council literary fellowships (one for fiction, one for nonfiction), two Will Rogers Medallion Awards, and three Spur awards from Western Writers of America. His most recent books are *Good Water* and *Destiny at Dry Camp*, frontier novels with Five Star.

The employees of Five Star Publishing hope you have enjoyed this book.

Our Five Star novels explore little-known chapters from America's history, stories told from unique perspectives that will entertain a broad range of readers.

Other Five Star books are available at your local library, bookstore, all major book distributors, and directly from Five Star/Gale.

Connect with Five Star Publishing

Visit us on Facebook:
  https://www.facebook.com/FiveStarCengage

Email:
  FiveStar@cengage.com

For information about titles and placing orders:
  (800) 223-1244
  gale.orders@cengage.com

To share your comments, write to us:
  Five Star Publishing
  Attn: Publisher
  10 Water St., Suite 310
  Waterville, ME 04901